Praise
THE NEW A~~MERICAN~~

"[Marcom's] telling resonates with he~~art~~ spite the travails she is describing, Marcom's writing is vibrant and often poetic.... Today's headlines will not let us forget that thousands of other children are still riding the Bestia. Marcom's compassionate novel illuminates their painful journey."

—*NEW YORK JOURNAL OF BOOKS*

"[An] emotionally piercing, compulsively readable novel."

—*SAN FRANCISCO CHRONICLE*

"[Marcom] depicts inhumanity with visceral force, but her bracing empathy (and hope) shines above all."

—*ENTERTAINMENT WEEKLY*

"Inspired in part by interviews with Central American refugees, and told in lyrical prose, Micheline Aharonian Marcom's novel *The New American* tracks the heart-pounding and fictional journey of a dreamer, a term referring to young undocumented immigrants who were brought to the United States as children, who have lived and gone to school here, and who, in many cases, identify as American."

—*FORTUNE*

"We need books like *The New American*, by Micheline Aharonian Marcom, which sweeps you into an uncomfortable reality, expands your heart, and helps you see through the eyes of a dreamer fighting to regain a lost promise. The world within its pages is unflinching and cruel but brims with hope and beauty. A catalyst for connection and empathy, *The New American* is also an immersive page-turner that will keep you reading eagerly to its conclusion."

—*NECESSARY FICTION*

THE NEW AMERICAN

Micheline Aharonian Marcom

SIMON & SCHUSTER PAPERBACKS

New York London Toronto Sydney New Delhi

Simon & Schuster Paperbacks
An Imprint of Simon & Schuster, Inc.
1230 Avenue of the Americas
New York, NY 10020

First Simon & Schuster trade paperback edition August 2021

SIMON & SCHUSTER PAPERBACKS and colophon are registered trademarks of Simon & Schuster, Inc.

For information about special discounts for bulk purchases, please contact Simon & Schuster Special Sales at 1-866-506-1949 or business@simonandschuster.com.

The Simon & Schuster Speakers Bureau can bring authors to your live event. For more information or to book an event, contact the Simon & Schuster Speakers Bureau at 1-866-248-3049 or visit our website at www.simonspeakers.com.

Interior design by Wendy Blum

1   3   5   7   9   10   8   6   4   2

Library of Congress Cataloging-in-Publication Data has been applied for.

ISBN 978-1-9821-2072-6
ISBN 978-1-9821-2073-3 (pbk)
ISBN 978-1-9821-2074-0 (ebook)

For those who made and those who make the journey
For those who did not survive it, que en paz descansen

For my son

I have caused thee to see it with thine eyes, but thou shalt not go over thither.

Deuteronomy 34:4

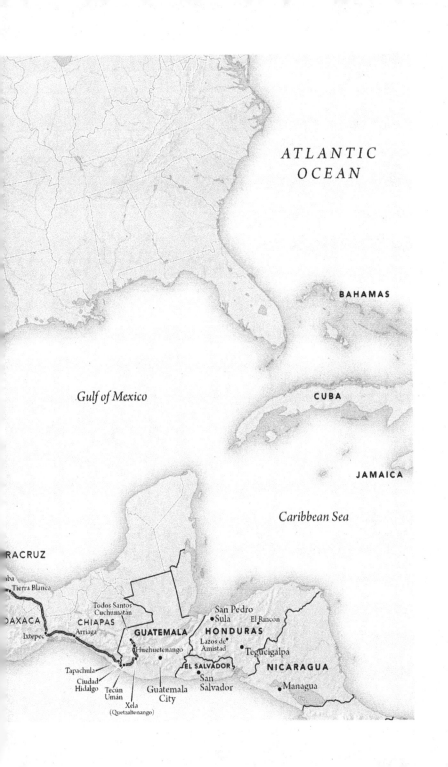

ATLANTIC
OCEAN

BAHAMAS

Gulf of Mexico

CUBA

JAMAICA

Caribbean Sea

RACRUZ

aba
Tierra Blanca

Todos Santos
Cuchumatán

San Pedro
•Sula

El Rincón

OAXACA

CHIAPAS

Ixtepec

Arriaga

GUATEMALA

HONDURAS

Tapachula

Ciudad
Hidalgo

Tecún
Umán

Xela
(Quetzaltenango)

Huehuetenango

Lazos de
Amistad

•Tegucigalpa

NICARAGUA

EL SALVADOR

San
Salvador

•Managua

Guatemala
City

Behold the girl and see how her brow illuminates the penumbra as if it itself were a source of light. She turns and in the dimness he can see the back of her head, the long dark hair, the two sharp lines of her scapula in relief against the fabric of her tee shirt. How long is the wait for the train? she says. The darkness lightens. They are at the railway yard and she is standing next to the steel rails; small whitegrey stones lie beneath her feet and the passengers' detritus—discarded papers, plastic bags, cigarette butts—is mixed among them. On the tracks behind her the bottom portion of a young boy's body lies prone, its stiff legs clad in torn blue jeans, its small feet shod in old tennis shoes. Milo, whose is it? she asks. The girl turns to face him and gazes directly into his eyes now and he can see her beauty more fully, its refulgence, and then, as if from an obscure room of his imagination, a sign: the horizontal line of her eyes (dark pupil to dark pupil) adjoins the vertical length made from nose to chin midway between her brows T. And behold the symbols, he thinks, and how they and all of our stories are dark phenomena of this dark earth.

THE NEW
AMERICAN

The Train

May 10, 2012

Here is a god more powerful than I am who, coming, will rule over me.

Dante Alighieri, La Vita Nuova

He is on the bus. The old Blue Bird school bus slowly climbs the steep and winding dirt road as it leaves the green misty valley of Todos Santos behind on its way to Huehuetenango two hours away, but he cannot see any of it through the windows in the darkness. In the seats near him, women hold their babies and toddlers and the old men hold their straw hats in their laps, bound chickens squawk and crik from their baskets overhead. The bus is filled with people of all ages and with their things tied up in big cloth sacks and cheap plastic bags. The engine is loud and cranks and the bus is crowded and cold and he wonders again how many days it will take to arrive and can I ever get it all back?

He had dressed carefully in the hour before dawn at his great-aunt's house in dark blue jeans, a long-sleeved shirt, a tee shirt beneath that, new white tennis shoes with a red stripe sewn onto their sides, and his red baseball cap. He grabbed his nylon jacket at the last moment, and although it is the beginning of the warmer rainy season in the Highlands, the old bus is damp and unheated, and he is glad he is wearing it. He had already decided to bring the silver wristwatch his mother gave him three years ago when he graduated from high school and he turns his left wrist and looks at it: 5:20 AM. He holds his small green backpack tightly on his lap.

Inside his old school pack he carries a plastic bottle of water, two lollipops he bought yesterday with his cousin's children from a market stall, a paperback novel, a new journal (where he plans to keep a record of this journey), and a ballpoint pen. He carries an extra tee shirt, two changes of underwear, one pair of white athletic socks, a toothbrush, some paste, and a small piece of hard soap he had wrapped in a scrap of paper. He has four hundred dollars U.S. hidden beneath the insoles of his tennis shoes, two hundred in each shoe, all of what had remained in his bank account in California, and three hundred quetzales tucked into one of the pockets of his blue jeans. He carries another forty dollars in the other pocket along with a small color photograph of her folded between two ten-dollar bills. He thinks of the things he now carries on this bus and of what he left behind in Todos Santos: several pairs of blue jeans, tee shirts, the traditional red-striped pants and handwoven shirt his aunt purchased for him upon his arrival in town two-and-a-half weeks ago (without it, Emilio, you won't look like one of our men, she'd said), a second pair of tennis shoes, three books he was assigned at university last term, his school ID, his old mobile telephone, his bank card. He thinks of his cash, his silver watch, the red cap and green pack and the book and journal and pen and how some things transit the earth easily and others do not. And he thinks how Aunt Lourdes will soon rise from her bed and discover his absence when she doesn't find him in the main room on the sleeping pallet she borrowed from her eldest son, Anselmo. How she will walk next door and give Anselmo the news and his cousin will thereupon phone Berkeley and how his mother and sisters in Berkeley will begin to worry, as perhaps will she if she is apprised of it. Yet even so he will not call or contact his family or his girlfriend until he has made it a good distance from here: his mind is set on this course of action and he will follow it. And the winch he has imagined took residence inside him last February, ponderous and metallic, abutting his

4

sternum, turns and pulls a wire from his bowels toward his stomach until his throat also cinches and he puts his hand into the jeans pocket with the quetzales and finds and fingers the white stone Antonia found for him on a beach in Northern California four months ago and he carries it back with him to the North.

He saw her standing atop the low seawall. Light brown hair pulled back into a ponytail, long legs in tight blue jeans, and a smile of hello in her blue eyes. She looked happy. He shouted out to her not to go into the ocean because the tide was unpredictable and she might drown. She replied that it was safe and warm and that she was a strong swimmer and she jumped off of the low seawall fully clothed into the water below and although they were at Muir Beach the sea looked different, calmer and darker blue, abutting the stones. He felt suddenly terrified and yelled out her name, but he didn't jump into the water after her because of the paralysis the terror caused in his body and the tide rose and took her from him. She was saying something he couldn't hear as she drifted farther and farther out, wave upon wave, to another place in the long distance, and he felt again his grief and rage and loneliness. He wanted to follow after her, he thought perhaps she might drown, but he remained where he was next to the seawall. He saw the back of her head like the head of a small sea lion far out in the dark blue water, near the light blue sky, as she drifted now onto the widest part of the ocean. Where has she gone? he thought.

Emilio awakens as the bus pulls into the parking lot of the busy terminal in Huehuetenango and cuts its engine. The sun has risen in the sky and lights up the brightly painted yellow concrete building and the dozens of red, blue, and green Blue Bird busses parked in front of it; people mill about everywhere he can see. He disembarks amid the commotion of engines and travelers and hawkers selling their wares and asks around for buses to Xela. An older ladino driver tells him the next one will not come for at least an hour because one just departed.

How long does it usually take from Huehue?

Depends on how fast you take the pass, the driver says. Three, four hours.

Emilio finds a place to sit and wait next to a man and his wife on a small bench near the open doorway inside the terminal. He takes off his nylon jacket, unzips his bag and pulls out *Great Expectations* and a yellow lollipop, and he stashes the jacket inside the pack. The candy is sweet and assuages his hunger, but he realizes after staring at the same page for several minutes that he is too unsettled to read and he puts the novel away again and hopes time will pass quickly while sugary saliva fills up his mouth.

He looks around at the old abandoned ticket stalls, at the cracked tile floor, at the light blue paint peeling off of the dirty, stained walls of the waiting area. He sees the old, the middle-aged, adolescents and small children, indigenous and ladino travelers sitting and standing and walking around. He can hear the revving of the brightly painted school busses when their engines start up and their belts begin to whir loudly; he can make out some of the busses' monikers through the open doorway in the bright sunlight. The names are painted in large, black cursive letters across the top portion of each windshield, *Esmerelda Mi Amor, Mi Pepa*. He bites off a piece of hard yellow sucker and as he chews it he wonders idly about the American schoolchildren who rode around in these very busses (maybe I took one to Jefferson Elementary a decade ago?) in American cities years before they were retired from use and sold down here and re-painted, retooled, and given individual names in preparation for intrastate travel.

Within the hour most of the busses depart and the terminal empties of most of its passengers. In the temporary lull Emilio notices an indigenous hawker walking around with a large burden of goods. Clay necklaces and stone bracelets hang from her thin arms, colorful wool blankets stack high onto her left shoulder, and a red-and-green-striped rebozo slung across her other shoulder holds a small hump of a child at her back. The child's head and most of its body are covered by the fabric, and two bare feet dangle down the small lady's spine. The blanket-seller passes in front of him now saying necklaces señor, bracelets for your señora, as if an entreaty. He shakes his head no and she petitions him again and not until the third failed appeal does she turn and walk deeper into the terminal building offering her goods to the air. Emilio thinks for a moment he can hear something else retreating in space with her form, softly interpolating her continual refrain, but then it, like she, moves out of earshot.

He continues to watch the blanket-seller. She lifts her jewelry-laden arms toward an old man next without any luck and she then approaches a young couple, a group of older women, and finally a mother and two small children who are eating their lunch at another bench across the sala. Emilio sees the mother extend her hand toward the blanket-seller and he thinks finally she has made a sale. The blanket-seller turns back and heads toward him again with her load and the unmoving red-and-green hump. She kneels down on the cracked tiles not five feet away and removes first the high stack of blankets from her shoulder, then the necklaces and bracelets from her arms, and she unknots the rebozo last, takes its weight from her body and unwraps a child on the floor. A small, slight boy in a tattered tee shirt and short pants emerges from the red cloth. He could be two, or perhaps three years old, Emilio thinks (in Todos Santos he had quickly learned most children were smaller and looked younger for their age than he was used to). The boy sits next to the pile of colorful blankets and blinks slowly as his eyes accustom to the light. His short black hair appears matted; a sheen of dried yellowgreen snot covers his nose and mouth. Emilio watches the blanket-seller as she now tears a piece of meat from a chicken leg she holds in a paper napkin in her hand; the boy has already opened his mouth and she puts the meat inside it. The boy looks around while he chews. When he finishes he looks back again at his mother who offers him another portion and she then takes some for herself. The boy moves his lower jaw up and down several times and then opens his mouth again widely (like a chick, Emilio thinks) and she presses a small piece of yellow tortilla against his bottom lip and tongue.

As the seller and her son finish eating the food the young mother of two shared with them from her own family's repast, Emilio realizes in its absence what had been its source: the boy is no longer making it, filling the lowest chambers of my hearing (which sounds my mind did not fully register or comprehend) with the offbeat engine of his moans, the low continuous cries he made. The sound has quit the terminal and now I also understand its cause: hunger.

The blanket-seller stands up and restraps the quiet child to her back, reloads her wares, and resumes her sales. A blanket for you, señor? she asks him this time.

No, no, thank you. I'm traveling a long distance, he says.

And the morning light expands further while he continues to wait. A bus for Xela should arrive in another fifteen minutes, Emilio overhears the man next to him say to his companion.

An hour later My Baby quickly fills up. Emilio finds an open seat in one of the last rows next to two women dressed in their traditional clothing, glad he won't stand in the aisle for hours like the passengers who are boarding after him. The two women each hold a large round bundle wrapped in handwoven cloth on their laps and he wonders what they might carry inside it while they travel.

Two foreigners, one blonde and the other brown-haired, step up and pay the attendant their fare at the front of the bus and begin to look for a seat. They are speaking to each other in loud voices and they are taller, fatter, pinker-skinned, and loosely limbed compared to the shorter and circumspect black-haired locals who surround them. Two men four rows ahead of Emilio stand up and offer their seats to the foreigners, and the girls thank them profusely with several strongly accented graciases. Each girl now removes an enormous rucksack from her back and tries to find room for it in the overhead storage area and the same men who gave up their seats assist them. Emilio can't make out what one is saying to the other, but he knows without hearing their words distinctly that they are Americans. They look it. They are the first Americans he has seen since he was deported from the Bay Area, and as he watches them adjust their belongings and settle into their seats, he realizes how much he wants to talk to them. He has liked seeing their familiar clothes and gestures and features on this local bus. He has missed the cadences of English and the everyday ease of speaking it.

The bus soon departs the station and within fifteen minutes they are on the Pan American Highway. Emilio asks the lady next to him if she will guard his seat for a moment and she nods a yes. He dons his small green pack and makes his way toward the girls, squeezing by the people standing in the aisle, including the two men who gave up their seats and who look at him strangely but say nothing as he moves past them. When he is within reach of the blonde, he taps her on one shoulder and watches as she grabs the hanging neck pouch she wears underneath her tee shirt (he can see the telltale sign of its strap around her neck), which doubtless carries her passport and other valuables. How's it going? he says loudly, and both she and the other girl turn their heads sharply toward him. A look of surprise alters the nervous masks of their faces as they put him and his speech together. He smiles easily and tells them his name and asks theirs and reaches for the metal stanchion of the seat adjacent to them to keep from falling as the bus lurches and picks up speed. He notices the blonde releases her tight grip on the neck pouch.

You speak English perfectly, she says.

My parents are from Guatemala but I grew up in Northern California.

I'm Kristen, the other girl says.

Oh sorry, I just assumed you were from here.

It's no problem. Where are you guys from?

Chicago, the blonde says. We've been in Antigua for ten days taking a course at La Unión Spanish School. What about you?

Two and a half weeks.

Are you visiting family?

Yes.

That's nice.

People here are so nice, Kristen says, and everything is so cheap! We can't stop buying things to take back with us. But you've probably been here before, so I guess you know that already.

Yes, of course, he says. There are a lot of cheap and beautiful things made in this country.

By now the bus is throwing him from side to side and he begins to feel nauseated.

I think I should go sit back down, it looks like we are starting to climb. Maybe we'll see one another in Xela?

Kristen smiles and says that would be so great, and the blonde also shows him her symmetrical and straight white teeth. Emilio returns to his seat and the lady dressed in her traditional huipil with its purple and yellow geometric design nods at him again as he sits back down. The girl next to her, whom he assumes must be her daughter and who is wearing an identical handwoven blouse, has already fallen asleep. The old metal bus is now filled with loud recorded music and lulls him. He closes his eyes and although he is tired, he finds he cannot sleep. He notices the tightening in his bowels and stomach and chest once more and he realizes that he hates the two girls he just spoke with, girls he would have found superficial or merely silly only a few months ago. Hates their pink fat smiling rich bodies on this loud old dilapidated American bus. Hates that they can proceed from here to there with their correct identification papers tucked into hidden neck pouches, in and out of towns and across international borders, thinking only of exotic things they might buy and of Indians they could meet along their path while they learn to say ¿cuánto cuesta? at a Spanish language school, and he himself cannot. They will board an airplane soon and go home, he thinks, and although an airplane brought me it will not take me back and so I can only go like this. And while he knows that he is being unreasonable, that the reasons he is on this bus traversing Guatemala have nothing in fact to do with the nice white girls, still his hate and envy of the Chicagoans exceed him and he finds he cannot sleep or relax, the bus loud and rumbling, the diesel fumes filling up his mouth.

The bus arrives at the crowded terminal in Xela just after noon. As Emilio steps down onto the pavement he sees the two American girls wearing their heavy packs and waiting for him.

Hey, so, do you want to hang out in town? Kristen says, friendly and welcoming.

We could have lunch together, where are you staying? the blonde asks. We are going to look for a hotel for the night and drop off our packs and then get something to eat.

I'd love to, he says, but I'm meeting friends in a half hour.

Are you heading into town? Our guidebook says it's a fifteen-minute walk.

They're picking me up here, he says.

The girls look disappointed as they smile their goodbyes and head toward the city center. Emilio walks inside the terminal to ask a ticket vendor about busses to Tecún Umán and learns one doesn't depart until eight p.m. He decides he should go into town after all and get something to eat but now worries he'll see the girls on the street and they'll know he lied to them and he's not even sure why he did. I can say my plans changed at the last minute, he thinks, that I'm meeting my friends later tonight, and somehow this ready story bolsters him. He waits twenty minutes, however, before he begins the half-mile walk to the downtown to make certain he won't overtake them.

The main avenue of Calzada Independencia is filled with old die-sel pickup trucks, a handful of shiny new ones, small passenger cars, big transport trucks for water and soda, motorcycles, scooters, and the ubiquitous colorfully painted Blue Bird busses. All of the vehicles scream by him, honking, crossing over the lines between lanes at random, moving in a frenzy, pouring out black exhaust smoke and somehow not hitting one another in the seeming chaos. He walks alongside the thoroughfare until he reaches cobblestoned streets and eventually the edge of the central plaza and a large metal sign:

WELCOME TO XELA. GUATEMALA'S
SECOND-LARGEST CITY. ONE OF THE OLDEST
SETTLEMENTS IN THE K'ICHE'-MAYA REGION!

A massive white cathedral rises high above the other buildings in the large plaza. A tall green and black volcano towers higher above everything else in the mountains beyond.

He stops at a food stand and buys a Coca-Cola and a sandwich. He's still not very hungry, only tired, but he knows he should eat something since he won't arrive at the border with Mexico until late tonight. He looks for an empty park bench in the plaza where he can eat his lunch and sees one in front of the National Bank past an old woman kneeling on a blanket on the ground. As he walks past the beggar she says something to him he cannot understand and he stops and asks her pardon in Spanish. I don't speak K'iche', he says, and only a few words of Mam.

Where from? the beggar asks in heavily accented Spanish.

The United States.

She lifts her thin arm and extends her hand toward him.

You have a little for me? she says.

Emilio sees the dark-brown leathery skin holding her arm bones loosely without any fat to soften its purchase, her torn and stained huipil, the open palm, and he reaches into his jeans pocket and pulls out some change and the white stone. He puts the stone back into his pocket and hands the beggar two quetzales.

She looks at the coin in her hand.

I'm sorry, he says, I'm traveling a long distance. I must be careful.

As he resumes walking toward the stone bench, he thinks he hears the beggar say something more although it is also possible he has imagined it.

Yes, careful, son. This country eats its children like a monster eats its young, for more than five hundred years.

Emilio opens the Coke and takes a long sip of the sweet carbonated beverage and decides to eat his sandwich later. He continues to the far end of the large plaza and sees two wide avenues leading off in different directions and several smaller streets with bright green- yellow- pink- and aquamarine-painted shops and restaurants. There are traditional food places, a few American fast-food joints, bakeries, tortillerías, a modern café, two other banks, clothing stores, a stationery store. On the narrowest streets, tall concrete walls shield the edifices from view, their flat tops covered in large pieces of broken green and clear glass bottles cemented together like so many rows of sharp menacing teeth. Private guards stand at attention with black assault rifles in front of the banks and an upscale boutique.

Here all the men dress in Western attire, and while many of the indigenous women wear their traditional clothes, others wear Western, and some a combination of both: the woven wraparound skirt and a tee shirt tucked in at the waist. He sees indigenous and he sees ladinos. He finishes the last of his Coca-Cola and he thinks how the sugar and caffeine have revived him; how in just half a day he has already made it to the department of Quetzaltenango; how all of this is new to him: the city, the architecture, the people. Guatemalan Spanish emits from TVs, radios, and from the mouths of shopkeepers and passersby and he hears K'iche', as he heard Mam in Todos Santos. I have never known any of it before and perhaps that is why, he thinks, these past weeks have seemed like something out of a dream. Of a remote mountain town with its own yellow and bright-green painted buildings. Of men and young boys walking the streets each morning in their handwoven red-striped pants with the firewood piled high onto their backs for the wood-burning stoves. Of my great-aunt making corn tortillas by hand once Anselmo brought the wood and she lighted it. Of cold air and smoke rising, roosters crowing throughout the day, chickens, turkeys, and stray dogs in the unpaved and paved roads, bands of children running around the plaza beneath colorful paper banners, and the marimba players entertaining the crowd for hours on Saturday during market day. Of the vomit on the stones the morning after the festivities. Of empty cans of Coke, Gallos, and discarded chip bags. Of the low-lying clouds and the verdant plots of maize interspersed with the trees in the mountains. Of the faces of strangers where I (strangely) saw my father again: his build and features, his carriage and soft-spoken manner; the way my mother wore her traditional blouses and skirts on special occasions (until she eventually began to wear only American clothes). Their accents, their diction, the sometimes stilted way they spoke their second and third languages (Spanish, English). My dad resurrected in the mouths of unknown men. It is unfathomable, yet oddly also familiar; but it is not mine, this is not me. I don't belong here, he thinks. And he feels again the out-of-placeness he has felt since he arrived with his old green backpack to Aunt Lourdes's house. It motivated him and it formulated a simple plan (northward, toward Mexico). It set up a meeting with Anselmo's friend,

Gustavo, who had gone north five years before about how to do it. It calculated what items to take in his pack, where to hide his money, how early to rise this morning and slip out of his aunt's house unnoticed and catch the local bus in the central square in the hours before dawn. It spoke the refrain, it remained lodged behind his lonely sternum, and pushing him, urged him, saying without surcease to the question in himself he cannot stop asking (can I ever get it all back?): *you must try.*

When he tires of wandering aimlessly he returns to the central plaza. The beggar and food vendors have all departed and the light of day is easing and dimming behind the clouds. He eats the sandwich he purchased earlier. He looks at the sky and the people walking by him who seem to have somewhere to go and he wishes he too had a destination nearby or that he knew someone in Xela and someone knew him. He would even be happy, he thinks, to see the girls from Chicago and talk about shopping or tourism or American television shows or the best eateries in town and share a meal. He doesn't see their familiar faces after all. He sits until the volcano in the distance begins to blacken after the disappearance of the sun behind it. When the light reddens and the high end of the sky begins to darken to a deeper blue, he stands up. 6:27 it says on his watch. The air has gotten cold again and he puts his nylon jacket back on.

He returns to the terminal and boards the bus at eight-thirty. The ride to Tecún Umán will take three and a half hours and he is glad he thought to purchase a bag of chips from a vendor in front of the station. It is night. The bus engine is loud and the music plays loudly and the bus moves quickly along the highway, leaning heavily this way and that, while the passengers doze or sit quietly. A few babies' cries occasionally punctuate the air.

As the bus moves north the air becomes warmer and he removes his jacket and later his long-sleeved shirt. He eats the chips and the second lollipop for his dinner. He finishes his bottled water. He closes his eyes to the night.

He walked in a vast desert and the sharp thorns of cacti pushed through the soles of the cheap plastic sandals he wore. His feet and ankles tore and he felt blood running out of the wounds. The ocotillo and mesquite scratched his arms and face, and a creosote plane spread out before his eyes. How far is it, he asked, where are you going? She was walking ahead of him in the near distance and he could see although it was night and although it was unlighted. She was naked. He saw her light-brown hair, her lovely body: the long thin legs and narrow hips and wide shoulders and then the flat plane of her belly and her small breasts. She was a runner and she had been running across the hot sand. Her bright body flew ahead of him like a flash of light across the western sky. A beacon.

We will reach the southern border soon! she called out. Do you still love me?

Then his father appeared before him and he looked robust as he had before he got sick and too thin. Son, his father said, it is just a bit farther. Don't forget the migra are mosquitoes and to bring your red hat, it will protect you during the hot days from the hot sun, one hundred and eighteen degrees in summer. They will bite. And remember to fill up your water bottle.

Papá, he said, you have not died any longer?

Chht. He startles and opens his eyes and checks that his green pack is still secure on his lap and all the zippers are sealed tight. Everything is okay. He looks at his watch and sees it's almost midnight as the bus turns into a small outdoor depot with one streetlamp illuminated in front of a metal awning. Through the window he can see four scantily dressed young girls in high heels standing beneath a ficus tree in the otherwise empty terminal. The passengers slowly disembark and Emilio breathes in the warm night air for a moment when he steps down. He approaches one of the girls, her dark eyes covered over in dark makeup, her black hair loose down her back, and he asks her if she knows of a reasonably priced hostel nearby. She says four blocks away on 5th Street there are several, and points in the direction he should walk.

I can show you the way? she says.

Sorry, I have a girlfriend, he says.

The young girl laughs and the top row of her silver metal-capped teeth flashes briefly inside the shadows the leaves of the ficus make.

Emilio walks quickly in the darkness of the new moon night, worried about the dollars in his shoes and the unfamiliar streets of Tecún Umán. He sees a streetlamp ahead of him and eventually a sign for the Tikal Residence. He pushes the buzzer on the intercom by the metal door.

Do you have anything for tonight?

How many are you?

One.

I only have a bed in a room with three others. Thirty quetzales.

Yes, okay, he says. He thinks: I'm tired, it's late, I want to lie down.

A bare-chested boy in shorts and plastic sandals opens the door and says this way. Emilio walks up a dim stairwell to the second-floor landing where a fat middle-aged man waits and takes a quick and close look at him. The fat-bellied man nods him into his office, which is little more than a room with a metal folding chair and a small wooden table and an old television on the top of it. A freestanding oscillating fan runs on high speed from one corner, but the room is nonetheless hot and stuffy. The TV is tuned to a syndicated American police show dubbed into Spanish.

Pay now, the manager says.

Emilio reaches into his pocket and takes out a fifty quetzales bill and hands the money over, relieved it isn't too expensive.

It's the last door on your left at the end of the hallway. The three in there are already sleeping, but one of the bunk beds is still unoccupied. If you want to shower in the morning, it'll be seven more. The manager hands him his change and goes back to watching his television show.

Emilio walks down the dimly lit hallway that smells strongly of insect repellant and mold and he finds and opens the door the manager had indicated. Three heads pop up from their beds.

What do you want? one says. From his accent Emilio can tell he's not Guatemalan or Mexican.

I paid for a night.

26

Okay, idiot, then come in quickly and close the door. We've been up for nearly twenty hours. With that the man turns over and goes back to sleep and the other two heads relax again beneath the shells of their blankets.

Emilio climbs up onto the top bunk he saw was empty when the door opened and let in a quadrangle of light. He can feel a foam mattress and a blanket beneath him in the darkness, but no sheets. He takes off his backpack and puts it at the head of the bed to use as his pillow and he takes off his shoes and puts them next to him by the wall. He removes his red baseball cap. He lies on top of the blanket and it smells rank and musty and he says goodnight to himself inside of himself and closes his eyes. In that darkness he sees her before him: blue-eyed and smiling. And then, inevitably, as they have each night for the past two and a half weeks other images rise in his mind as if on a documentary reel, and he sees his mother and sisters inside their house on Carleton Street, his bed with its large grey coverlet, the living room and its west-facing bay window to the tree-lined street. The loop continues and includes his Aunt Lourdes tonight and her concrete two-room abode, how she tried to make him feel welcome and comfortable despite his low spirits, and Anselmo who said that in time he'd get used to the life here. I'll show you, cousin, how to prepare the soil for maize, I'll take you up the sacred mountain, he promised, as his two young children ran around them in circles in the central plaza, the long white sticks of their lollipops dancing up and down in their mouths.

Emilio tries to put the images out of his mind into another room down the long hallway of his imagination (he closes the door), and get some sleep. For a brief moment, however, he wishes he too were a believer like his mother and sisters and great-aunt and his cousin Anselmo and that he might pray and ask for particular outcomes. It is hot and stuffy in the room and he can hear the man who chastised him earlier snoring softly from the lower bunk. But he cannot, because he has never believed in God.

Listen, she said, listen to me: I've never felt this way before. Why are you laughing? It's true. Most college guys are idiots: they just want to drink beer and fuck. When you and I make love there is nowhere else on earth I'd rather be than here in this small bed in this small dormitory room at UC Berkeley. It's real. And the portent of our bodies. Since November when we first met at Café Strada . . . You are laughing again! I'm going to get up, get dressed. I want to go for a run on the fire trail and you said we could meet later at the library and study together for our midterm exams?

Antonia got up and vanished. And the whole world vanished.

In the morning he hears the three travelers moving around the room. The sun has not yet risen fully but the room is lightening. He looks at his watch: 6:08 AM.

He sees them leave with their backpacks: there are two men and a girl with black hair with blonde highlights dyed into it. He turns over and tries to go back to sleep. The blanket beneath him is dark brown, but he thinks he can make out the image of an enormous lion's head printed on it in yellow and orange.

At eight o'clock he finally gets up and takes a shower. On his way out of the hostel he stops in the manager's office again and asks the way to the river.

You're crossing over too, the manager says, and laughs and goes back to watching his television show.

Emilio heads toward the town center to find a place to get breakfast. He goes into the first restaurant that looks clean and inexpensive and orders a plate of scrambled eggs with tomatoes, black beans, fried plantains, and thick handmade corn tortillas, similar to what his mother sometimes prepared on weekends. This morning he is hungry, and he quickly devours his food and drinks a cup of sweetened black coffee while the day outside slowly heats up.

He pays and leaves the restaurant and begins to wander aimlessly. The streets are busy and filled with pickup trucks, old two-door sedans, and hundreds of bicycle taxis that herd people and things around the town and across the bridge to the border with

Mexico and back again. The sun is not yet at its zenith and it is already hot and the air is thick; the back of his short-sleeved shirt is damp beneath his green pack. He walks by dozens of bars and food stands, Mexican music plays from car radios and freestanding radios, and here everyone wears Western attire; the women twist their long black and brown hair into tight knots at the napes of their necks or high onto their heads with sharp plastic hair-fasteners.

Emilio is hot and bored and nervous. He wishes for a moment he had his mobile telephone and that he could text his friends like he would if he were at home, and Antonia, as if everything were normal. Eventually he returns to Restaurant Las Vegas and asks for a Coca-Cola and sits and watches a television in the corner without much interest. An American sitcom plays, one he watched as a boy, where three men raise a child by themselves. He is still hot and sweating and the restaurant's overhead fan does little to cool him. He tries to read his book but like yesterday finds it difficult to focus on the words before him. His cola has quickly warmed to room temperature and because he declined the ice the waitress offered (he worried the tap water might not be clean) he sips at the now unappealing sweet soda. He looks at the other patrons eating their meals and conversing easily with one another. Eventually he pulls the journal and ballpoint pen out of his backpack.

DAY 2

May 11. Tecún Umán.
3,000? miles.

He stares at the paper for a time but he doesn't write more. It is now after two o'clock and he pays the waitress for the soda. He leaves the half-full bottle of Coke on the table and goes outside onto the street and walks toward the river to see it up close.

The Suchiate divides Guatemala from Mexico and from where he stands appears to be no more than two hundred yards across. The muddy banks are littered in old plastic water bottles, soda bottles, plastic bags, and colorful discarded food wrappers. The brown-grey river is so shallow at this juncture a man can walk across it and not wet his hair.

Emilio watches as dozens of slipshod rafts made from wooden planks lashed to giant black inner tubes crisscross the expanse: they fill the small distance between the two countries with their transit as they carry goods and people to-and-fro and to again. A raftsman stands at the rear of each of the flatboats with a long pole and pushes it forward. The tall mountains of Mexico rise green and lush above everything in the distance. The international bridge and official point of entry spans the river not one hundred yards away.

The heat becomes more oppressive and Emilio finds a spot of silver shade to avoid the sun and continue observing the river traffic. Raftsmen return with goods piled high onto their wooden boards: tin cans, boxes of dry goods, beer, toilet paper, soda. The men look young and strong, their arms taut and muscular, as they demand payment in their bare feet and shorts while they load their passengers to return to the Mexican side. From what Emilio can tell by their accents, only Mexicans transport loads between the two nations. Two dollars to the other side, they say. They take and return passengers and things continuously from Guatemala to Mexico and back again.

Farther down the riverbank, he notices several half-naked men stepping into the river, each with a tall stack of plastic gasoline canisters strapped to his back. Emilio watches as they wade across the water with a walking stick as their balance; the enormous yellow jugs rising high above their heads, eventually they block the men's naked torsos to his eye.

Gas is cheaper in Mexico, the old man sitting next to him in the shade of the palm tree says when Emilio asks him what the porters are doing with the plastic canisters.

They buy in Hidalgo so as to not pay the customs.

It's worth so much effort? Emilio asks.

They can earn six, seven dollars a day if they make enough trips, the old man says.

Emilio watches two men now returning from the other side. Their backs bend double with the increasing weight of the filled canisters as they slowly descend from the river (like giant primordial insects emerging from the old chaos, he thinks). The sweat pours down the porters' faces from their labor; the tight muscles of their thighs contract and release.

It's decent work but only for the young ones, the old man says. My back and feet gave out years ago.

Emilio looks down at the old man's calloused splayed feet in his plastic sandals, at the thick, cracked discolored toenails.

Do you want one?

The old man pulls a pack of cigarettes out of his pocket. He looks up at Emilio.

Emilio says he doesn't smoke but thank you, and he notices how the old man's dark eyes have lightened to a muted grey from the slowly blinding cataracts of old age. He thinks how they must cloud his vision.

A woman in a red tee shirt approaches the river's edge and stops beneath another tree in the shade not too far from him and the old man. She looks like the girl from the hostel; Emilio recognizes the black hair and in it the dyed blonde strands. He can see that she is pretty, slim, young, and of medium height, and her breasts and hip bones push softly against her cotton tee shirt and jeans. She looks hot and her face is closed, her thin, light-brown arms dangle loosely from the bones of her shoulders.

Emilio takes leave of the old man and walks over to the girl. He introduces himself, he is not sure why he does it. She looks toward him and she is tense and tired, he can see, her eyes are a little puffy and red, and he thinks how she is very pretty nonetheless.

We shared the same room last night, I arrived after you and your companions had already gone to sleep.

She continues to look at him with anxious dark eyes that assess him carefully.

I'm also traveling north.

Nice to meet you, she finally replies in a quiet, subdued voice.

He asks her name and she pauses for another long moment. She begins to twist her hair between her index and second fingers.

I'm Matilde, she finally says.

It's a pleasure. Where are you from?

From around here, and you?

My parents are from a town six hours to the southeast, in the Highlands. But I grew up near San Francisco in the north of California.

Is that why you kind of talk like an American?

I guess so. He laughs. Why don't you talk like a chapín if you're from here? He smiles at her, he can't seem to help himself.

She laughs at that, and something in her relaxes and she lowers her hand from her hair and says she is from Tegucigalpa, Honduras, and that she's waiting for her friends to join her momentarily.

How long have you been on the road?

Four days, counting today. We stayed an extra night in Guatemala City.

It feels like I've been traveling a long time but I left only yesterday. Where are you headed?

She lifts her hand to her dark hair again and twisting it says, Arizona. Do you know it?

No. It's more than eight hundred miles from where I grew up.

She looks at him blankly.

More than a thousand kilometers.

A thousand? she asks.

The United States is a big country, he says, and smiles again.

By yourself? she says suddenly.

Yes. You're traveling with the other two?

We're four. Jonatan joined us today. My brother-in-law, Pedro, has crossed twice before and Jonatan went once, so they know the way.

She doesn't say anything else and they both watch as a raft

approaches with five Guatemalan women. When it reaches the riverbank, the women step onto the dirt with their purchases and head toward town. She looks across the river.

Have you been there? she asks, breaking the silence.

No, never.

Another raft of shoppers arrives and lets its passengers off with their bags of goods.

People talk about the difficulties, she says, and she lifts her chin slightly toward the opposite shore. But Pedro says he knows a good way. Here they are.

Emilio turns and sees three baseball-capped men walking toward him and Matilde, each of them carrying a black backpack. The oldest-looking one says, Matilde are you fine?

She says yes and introduces Emilio to her friends. He's returning to his house, she says.

Emilio extends his hand to Pedro, who shakes it firmly, and then toward Jonatan, who is the tallest of the group and smiles easily and looks like he could be in his late twenties. William is the youngest and mumbles a greeting without looking at him directly.

How are you going? Pedro asks Emilio.

I'm taking a bus from Hidalgo to Mexico City. Then from there I'll get another to the line.

You have your guide?

No, not yet, but I'll get one in the capital, or at the border.

There are police checkpoints along all the northern bus routes now. They ask for papers.

A friend told me how much to give the cops if they ask for my ID.

We have decided to take the cargo trains because it's much more economical! Jonatan jokes.

When are you going over?

After dinner. Then we'll walk to Tapachula, to the depot.

Can I join you on a raft?

Matilde is twisting and untwisting her hair again as they talk. William is silent and keeps his eyes on the ground, and Pedro says it's no problem. Jonatan teases, You never know, it might be useful to have someone along who can speak good English.

The group returns to the river before sundown after eating a meal at a sidewalk stand in the town center. The beef tacos with green onions, fresh radishes, spicy pickles and the cold sodas were cheap and tasted delicious, Emilio thinks, it must be because food tastes better when it is eaten with company.

Your features look Guatemalan, but you're a lot taller than most of the chapines I've met, Jonatan says. Did you eat a lot of hamburgers when you were a kid?

Jonatan walks next to him, the other three are several yards ahead.

I ate my share, Emilio laughs.

But, man, you move like a gringo, Jonatan says as he pats Emilio on the back. He smiles.

I do?

I saw it all in Phoenix when I was there six years ago: Mexicans, blacks, whites, Chinese, Chicanos who can't speak a word of Spanish, and a few catrachos like me who were just trying to get ahead!

How long did you live there?

I was in a restaurant for a little over a year and a half, washing dishes during the day, and at night I unloaded boxes in a warehouse. After I got picked up in a raid, they sent me back.

Did you learn any English?

Moderfokinbich.

The two men laugh.

Pedro turns and says come on, we need to get one.

The five approach the shore and Pedro asks around at various rafts for the price of portage for the group. Four dollars per person, the raftsmen say. They go up and down the riverbank looking for a better deal, but none will take them for less.

They charge us more if they can get away with it. We'll find a cheaper one, Pedro says. Keep some money accessible.

An adolescent pulls up to the shore and says he'll take them for two dollars each. Agreed on the price, the five settle onto the wooden slats of his raft.

This is my brother, the raftsman says, I'm taking him home for the night. Another teenager in shorts and a tee shirt wades into the water and joins them.

The sun is low in the sky and the redness begins to cover the green mountains. The light ascends orange then yellow and light blue toward the darkest blue of the bowl of the sky and the earth itself seems to begin to emit a darkness as night begins to come on. Emilio notices a tiny white sliver of moon hanging in the air.

The river green-blackens while their raftsman slowly pushes them across it. They can hear voices from dozens of other rafts moving on the water as they do. Hundreds of us are traversing it tonight, Emilio thinks. The air is still hot and humid, and he sweats as he has sweated all day. The dark river is calm and the stink of it rises onto the crepuscule as the artificial lights begin to come on on each side of the old waterway.

He sits next to Matilde, and like his companions he looks toward the Mexican town on the other shore. The raftsman pulls on his pole and the muscles in his arms work and strain, his stationary bare feet press against the splintery wood of their berth. The girl begins pulling on her hair, and Emilio thinks it must be her nervous habit to do so. He too feels the anxiety that must be in all of them.

Halfway across the river the raftsman abruptly stops his poling. You need to pay three more per person, he says.

Muchacho, Pedro says, we negotiated our passage at two.

It's the halfway tax, old man. Pay up or you can swim the rest of the way.

We had a deal, Pedro says.

The raftsman's brother pulls out a knife and threatens them with it.

Give us the money, or get the fuck off.

The Hondurans say that they don't know how to swim and they all pay the extra fare. Emilio doesn't want to get into the dark water or separate from the group, so he also gives the raftsman's brother three dollars. The raftsman's brother keeps his knife resting on his thigh until they reach their destination.

Welcome to Mexico, the raftsman says when they pull up onto the shore.

The five step off of the raft and into the thick, trash-strewn mud of Ciudad Hidalgo. They crush plastic water bottles and discarded cigarette butts and empty bags of potato chips as they climb the bank. They try in their manner to blend in with the other people on the street as they head into town, even though their backpacks and baseball caps and tense downturned faces give them away as foreigners.

You can try it with us if you'd like, Pedro says to Emilio.

Thank you, but I want to get a bus tonight, I'm in a hurry. Safe journey, and I hope you like Arizona, Emilio says to Matilde. It's hot, but at least it's not humid like here.

Be careful as you travel, she says.

He shakes the men's hands, and then hers. The four Hondurans head north and he walks alone toward the city center.

Ciudad Hidalgo is still bustling at this hour. The streets are jammed with food vendors and shops and loud music coming out of lighted-up shop and house windows. Pickup trucks and tricycle taxis fill the streets. Emilio keeps his head down and holds the straps of his green pack tightly. He stops for a moment at what looks like a main intersection to find someone and ask directions to the bus station.

A tricycle taxi pulls up next to him and the young driver asks him if he needs anything. Emilio asks the whereabouts of the terminal.

I can take you there if you want, the driver says. It's two kilometers from here.

How much do you charge?

I'm off duty, but it's on my way home. It's no problem, hop on.

The young driver wears a pressed shirt and shorts and looks to be about Emilio's age. He wears a black baseball cap with a purple and gold monogram for the Los Angeles Lakers and he smiles warmly.

The Lakers are my favorite team. You sure?

The driver laments their loss to the Dallas Mavericks in last year's finals and says it's no problem, get on.

Emilio climbs onto the covered bench of the tricycle taxi and they take off. In a few blocks, the taxi veers from the crowded street onto a small side street away from the city center.

Is the station at the edge of town? Emilio asks.

This is a shortcut.

The driver pedals strongly, his calf muscles bulge and strain, and they continue five more blocks and then turn onto another street moving even farther away from the downtown. Emilio asks again if the station is this way. The driver ignores him and peddles steadily. Emilio thinks perhaps he didn't hear his question but begins to feel uneasy as the town recedes farther and farther behind them. The hot wind covers his face. Has it been two kilometers already? Isn't that about a mile? Should I jump off?

Another few minutes pass and the driver abruptly stops the pedicab by a tall cement wall covered with colorful graffiti. We are here, get down, the young driver says.

A fallow cornfield lies on the other side of the road and the light is almost completely gone from the sky now. A small amount of red remains in the hazy clouds high above them. The earth blackens more by the minute.

Here? Where?

You heard me. Get off, asshole.

Emilio sees a car heading toward them on the road just as he steps down from the tricycle taxi. He can tell it's a police car from the telltale lights on the roof. The vehicle quickly pulls up beside them and stops and two cops get out: one is short and fat, and the other is of medium build.

Where are you from? the short fat cop says.

This guy brought me here for no reason, Emilio says.

The earth continues to blacken and the sky to dark-blue.

The taller cop walks up to him and punches him in the chest. He asked you where you are from, asshole, he says.

California, Emilio replies, as soon as he recovers his breath.

The fat cop laughs.

You lying fucker, the taller cop says, and hits him in the stomach this time. Emilio falls onto the dirt. The fat cop watches from where he stands; the young pedicab driver watches from where he sits.

You think you can come into Mexico without permission, without papers, you little shit?

I have almost thirty dollars I can give you.

What did you say, motherfucker? The taller cop begins kicking him in his stomach and back and Emilio puts his arms around his head to protect it.

That's all you've got?

Yes, he says, his voice trembling.

Check him, the fat cop says to the pedicab driver. The boy gets off of the bike and kneels next to Emilio and reaches into his front jeans pockets.

Here are the dollars, the pedicab driver says, and some quetzales.

Look in his backpack and check the waistband of his pants and his shoes, the fat cop says.

The boy searches the backpack and doesn't find anything he wants and then takes off Emilio's tennis shoes and searches underneath the soles and discovers the stashes of bills. Four hundred, the driver says after counting it.

Bring it here, the fat cop says, and grab the watch.

Is that it, faggot? the taller cop says, and begins to kick him again.

Yes, Emilio says. Yes, sir.

They lift him to his feet and shove him into the back seat of the police car. They throw his backpack and red baseball cap on top of him and the quetzales.

Take your bag and keep your Guatemalan money and don't say in Mexico we don't treat Central Americans with a certain restraint, the fat cop says.

Emilio overhears the taller cop tell the pedicab driver he can keep the new tennis shoes as a bonus. The night is fully drawn now. The cops drive Emilio to the border and across the international bridge, and dump him on the other side in Tecún Umán.

Don't come back, asshole, the fat one says.

They leave him on a sidewalk in the dark.

An older woman sees him limping along the main street, shoeless and lost, and tells him to go to the House of the Migrants. They will help you, she says, and she directs him the three blocks to it.

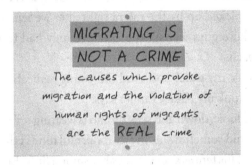

Emilio walks past the walls covered in posters warning of the dangers to migrants and past the sign, House of the Migrants, into an open lighted courtyard. I am a migrant, he thinks.

A volunteer opens the door a few minutes after he rings the bell. She says, My poor boy, come inside, and takes him to the main building to join the dozens of other migrants who are spending the night in the shelter. She tells him to write his name in the ledger and that later he can make a record of what happened in Mexico. Thank you very much, he says, and he hears how shaky and sad his voice sounds and thinks, is that me speaking?

Emilio walks into the dining area behind the volunteer and sees Matilde and Pedro drinking coffee at a long plastic table.

Matilde turns when she hears him say her name and stands up

and goes to his side. Pedro follows after her and she says, My God what did they do to you?

Are you okay, muchacho? Pedro asks.

Matilde places her hand on his arm and Emilio tells them how the two cops took all of his dollars and then dumped him back on this side of the border but what are you doing here, he asks, his voice still strange and uneven, but beginning to recover itself.

We got picked up by the migra right after we left you, Pedro says, but these guys weren't too bad. We only had to pay three hundred each.

They stole my watch too. And the young pedicab driver who tricked me took my Nikes, Emilio says.

Matilde looks down and sees Emilio is wearing only white athletic socks and somehow his overly mournful tone at the mention of the loss of his tennis shoes makes her smile a little. Emilio looks down and sees how ridiculous he looks in the dirty socks and he smiles also and asks, What happened to William and Jonatan?

They are getting cleaned up, Pedro says.

It's good to see you both again, Emilio says.

You too, she says, and she smiles more fully.

And Emilio thinks how bright her smile is, how she is even prettier when she does it.

Another volunteer directs him to a private room where she can give him medical attention. She uses antiseptic to clean the small cut on his face and hands and he shows her his chest and back where they kicked him and bruises are forming but his ribs fortunately do not appear to be broken, she says.

Would you like something to eat?

He says that he is not hungry, just sore and tired, and she directs him to the room where the migrants sleep.

The entire floor of the large dormitory room is covered with dozens of small foam mattresses. He sees Matilde lying between Pedro and Jonatan near the door, and he finds an empty mattress at the far end of the room. The shelter is predominantly filled with young men in their twenties and thirties, and the men talk and joke until the lights are turned off. The heat of the day is still upon him and on all of them in the room and he tries to sleep. His body aches and the shaking in his legs which began when they dropped him across the bridge diminishes finally as the pills the volunteer gave him take effect, and he begins to feel less pain. He holds his green backpack closely to his chest, happy to have most of the things he carried from his great-aunt's house and from California before that still with him, but he mourns the loss of his silver watch and the photograph of Antonia that he'd tucked in between his dollars. He puts his hands into his pocket and finds the white stone lying next to the quetzales. At least they didn't take everything, he thinks. He begins to feel drowsy and as he is falling into sleep he thinks how far everyone from home feels tonight (his old world, his old life) but the usual reel does not, for some reason, run its course inside his mind. The last thought he has is of Matilde and whether she too is hot and has fallen asleep yet or if she worries the night, pulls on her hair in the darkness where he and the others can no longer see it.

Do you like it, she said, and she pointed to her skirt and shirt. She was dressed in the traditional clothing of Todos Santos: the bright red handwoven huipil tucked into the dark blue wraparound skirt. Her long hair hung down her back in one large plait with orange ribbons woven through it. She looked beautiful, yet strange and foreign, and he began to take off her clothes. They were in her room again at the university dormitory. Don't ruin it, she said to him. When she was naked he took off his shirt and trousers and he desired her more than ever before, she is so lovely, he thought, and he lay on top of her body. She looked up at him and she was not Antonia now but someone else. This girl was dark-eyed and she said he ought to invite her to see the mountains and green slopes and the great valley of his ancestral homeland. Each sparrow rocking on the branches of pine and cypress and ficus.

Then they stood atop the highest peak and the cloud cover was a greywhite blanket covering the great valley and the town below them.

I only want to show you everything in the North, he said.

They sit at the long plastic tables in the dining area eating bowls of chicken soup and tortillas for lunch. Large ceiling fans run overhead but do little more than move the hot air around.

Emilio has bathed and washed his clothes and even shaved. He sits between Matilde and William and listens to Jonatan joking from across the table how despite all the evidence Mexicans still think they are the best soccer players in the world. Pedro is talking to two men at another table who were sent back from Mexico City to find out about new checkpoints.

I volunteered for lunch duty, Matilde says as she stands to take her dishes to the kitchen.

I'll help this shift, Emilio says, and follows after her.

Matilde begins washing the stacks of colorful plastic dishes. Emilio takes a rag and stands next to her and dries. They are quiet and working diligently and he is thinking how strange it is to be here with this girl in a shelter drying and stacking plates in northern Guatemala when only four weeks ago I was in an immigration detention center in Richmond, and a few months before that taking my final exams at UC Berkeley, living at home, working the register at the bakery on weekends, and falling in love with Antonia. He is stacking yellow bowls and red plates and thinking of the girl far away and of what lies ahead and his *can I ever get it all back* is still a progressive force upon him, no matter the corrupt cops yesterday and the young pedicab driver or his increased trepidation. It was only a little bad luck, he thinks. He looks at Matilde beside him who is focused intently on her task and he asks her why she is going up.

Why?

She looks in his eyes for a moment and then back down at the dishes in the soapy water. You seem better today, she says. Do you feel better?

I'm still a little sore, but a night's sleep has helped. Matilde, he says, it seems like not as many young women are going.

I have another question, she says.

She begins washing the silverware.

What?

Is it true that gringos prefer to eat inside their cars rather than inside the restaurant when they got to a Macdonal?

Don't make me laugh again, he says, laughing, when I do it hurts my ribs.

Once they've finished in the kitchen they go outside into the courtyard and sit beneath one of the large mango trees in the afternoon shade. The men near them are playing cards and checkers or dozing, and he sees how Matilde is twisting her hair next to him as she watches a card game. Emilio feels tired again and thinks he will take a short nap. He leans back in the plastic chair and crosses his arms and just as he closes his eyes he notices the lighter band of skin on his left wrist in the place where his silver wristwatch used to wrap around and cover it.

Later that day he gives a volunteer the details about the extortion and beating in Ciudad Hidalgo.

Do you want to make an official complaint against the municipal police?

No, he says. It's for your records only: two Mexican policemen and their pedicab driver accomplice. They took over four hundred dollars, my watch, and a pair of new tennis shoes.

If you are willing to denounce them, the volunteer says, we are gathering reports of abuse by the authorities, and while we haven't yet been successful, the father says we must keep trying. You could file an official complaint, or if you were willing to stay and testify?

I'm sorry, I can't, Emilio says, for he made his mind up last night about his next course of action.

He finds Pedro with a few migrants near a small old color television tuned to a soccer game. The heat is oppressive and many of the men have removed their shirts. Several closely follow the match.

Avoid the tracks near Tapachula, he hears a Salvadoran say to Pedro when he sits down next to him in an empty chair. Delinquents lie in wait behind the abandoned cars. Chiapas is filled with them now, and the police shake everyone down in Arriaga as always.

The police in Mexico are sons of bitches, no different than at home, the man sitting on the other side of the Salvadoran says.

But here without papers we are more fucked, the Salvadoran says. Narcos and gangs control everything on the road now, not like in the old days.

One of the men watching the game adds, You can't trust Mexicans, they all have two faces.

They think the Creator made them better than us.

The group of men laugh.

Who still remembers two thousand and nine? the man watching the game says.

Two to one!

So beautiful!

The men continue giving warnings and Emilio sits with them until they turn to joking or yelling about the ongoing match, which is now a close contest. And when everyone stands up to leave because dinner has been called, Emilio gets Pedro's attention and asks him if he can join them as far north as the capital.

I'd rather not travel alone, he says.

The trains can be uncomfortable, you understand?

Pedro is looking at him steadily.

I need to get a good distance into Mexico before I can ask my mother for help, Emilio says, somehow feeling obligated to explain. She will want me to wait in Guatemala until my attorney can do something. But there's nothing my attorney can do for me and I need to get back in time for school in August. When I'm in the capital I know she'll help.

Okay, Pedro says, it's your decision, muchacho. We need to get some rest: the jump awaits us tomorrow.

After breakfast the next morning the father joins the travelers in the dining hall and speaks to them about the dangers and the delinquents and the kidnappings and the violence and the women, he says, who face the violation of their bodies, and you men also. He talks to them in their group of fifty and tries to discourage their crossing over.

Organized crime controls the routes and many policemen

work for them now, he says. In Mexico without papers, brothers, you will have little or no recourse, little or no protection.

But the father's blue eyes and his pity and the stories he records in this House of the Migrants cannot dissuade any from continuing his journey. Each man, each woman, carries the reasons in their pocket, and they are the reasons which make the decision and we must go north, father, they say, we put our faith in God. God accompanies me, father, He will care for us. They give their humble thank you to the father, for your kindness, they say, for shelter and food. Only God will be our guide.

And the father tells them how the poor are the great soul of the world and may He be with them always.

Twenty-five migrants leave the house afterward to continue their journey and Pedro, Matilde, Jonatan, William, and Emilio are among them.

The Suchiate in the morning is lighter brown and docile, and the humid fury of the day begins. They find a raftsman for two-fifty apiece and cross over, and together the five begin walking from Ciudad Hidalgo toward Tapachula. They carry their backpacks filled with some food and a plastic liter bottle of water the shelter volunteers gave them, and their change of clothes; Emilio still carries his unread paperback, journal, and ballpoint pen. It's at least twelve hours over the mountains to Bombilla, Pedro says. The sun lifts higher in the east, and they walk on dried grass and brown dirt and the mountains rise greener in the day. The dark-green trees carry blackbirds upon them and looking up Emilio can see more blackbirds turning in a circle above their heads. The heat and humidity are heavier with each hour, the blackbirds lazily move along and the five sweat and walk.

They stop at a small muddy stream in the afternoon and the Hondurans fill their empty water bottles using a tee shirt to filter out the sediment. Emilio says that he'll fill his bottle later when they get into a town and he can find a spigot. The men pull their baseball caps low onto their foreheads to shield their eyes from the sun and quickly eat some of the food they have brought. Emilio's feet are tired and the used tennis shoes they gave him chafe his feet and blisters form along the tops of his toes, on the pads of his toes, and on the balls of his feet, but he says nothing. We cannot stop walking for long, the place is uncertain, Pedro says, it is best to keep moving at all times in Chiapas.

And in Tapachula we will face the Beast! Jonatan says to the air above them.

The day runs out and they are walking and each man and the girl think of the step in front of their last step and to make their foot touch the dirt in front of them. Emilio is thinking about his mother and how his cousin must have called her by now and that she will be worried and not wanting to cause worry but not knowing any other option than this one, the *you must try*, and how she could not help him when he was jailed, no matter the money she spent on his attorney, and she cannot help him here either. His feet hurt in the old, too-small tennis shoes, some of the blisters have burst, and his legs are tired and he has sweated through his tee shirt and his mother will be praying at St. Joseph the Worker in the white nave after work, he knows, but he doesn't know where he is now or when he'll arrive, so he can only follow William, who follows Matilde, who is behind Jonatan, and Pedro is at the head of their line. We are nearing Tapachula, Pedro says. The green bushes brush against their bodies as the land begins to darken, the light to lessen in the sky, and they are weary and anxious now because of the waning light and their fear gives them renewed energy to walk farther, faster, each step as fast as Emilio's legs can make the stride, and foot down, foot up, ignoring thereby his fear, his feet, their chafe and burn. Just a little bit farther now, muchachos, Pedro says, we are close.

Two delinquents appear from the augmenting of the black land, from the growth of the night. They stand before them in a small clearing, each with a machete raised above his head.

Where do you think you're going motherfuckers, one yells.

The five turn to run and see three more youths behind them, one with a large knife and the other two with handguns pointed at them.

Take off your backpacks and put them in a pile, one of the delinquents with a gun orders.

The five remove their packs and place them on top of each other on the ground.

Now your clothes. Everything. You too, muchacha, the same delinquent says.

Matilde asks if that is really necessary in a quiet voice, and the short fair one with the knife goes up to her and grabs her by the hair and pulls it. He places the blade against her throat and says, Stupid bitch, do what he tells you or I'll cut you.

Please don't harm us, Pedro says with a bad attempt at a Mexican accent, we are from Hidalgo. We were just out for a walk.

Shut up, asshole, you think we're stupid? You're nothing but a Central American piece of shit, the leader with the gun says. He approaches Pedro, who has already removed his shirt, and says, Open your mouth, fatty. Pedro obeys and the man shoves the metal barrel inside his mouth.

Can you tell it's a real Mexican one? the delinquent says. Now suck it, pussy.

Pedro presses his lips around the gun.

The youth pushes the barrel farther down his throat and laughs as Pedro chokes and gags and snot runs out of his nose, saliva from his mouth, tears from his eyes. He finally pulls the handgun out of his mouth and orders them all to lie on the ground. Pedro is coughing and shaking but he manages to remove the rest of his clothes and puts them on top of the others.

Jonatan is already naked but when he hesitates for a moment

before lying down on the dirt, one of the boys with a machete reaches out and cuts him across the cheek.

You're lucky I didn't cut off your nose, pig, now get down on the ground.

William and Emilio lie next to Jonatan, and Emilio sees in his peripheral vision how Matilde is unclothed now except for pink underwear and a black bra. She begins to remove her bra when the fair one with a knife grabs her by the arm and tells her to wait. The two with the machetes are rifling through all of their clothes looking for money and throw a piece of chewing gum and scraps of paper and a hair fastener and his small white stone from the pockets of the five pairs of jeans on to the dirt. They begin to put everything else into large plastic garbage bags they have brought, including shoes, backpacks, and hats. The delinquent who put his gun into Pedro's mouth now grabs Matilde by the arm and pulls her after him down a smaller diverging path. She asks him to please not hurt her for the love of God as he pulls her away, and he says shut up, bitch, or I'll cut your tongue out of your mouth. The short fair one with the knife and the one who cut Jonatan's face with his machete follow after them and disappear from sight.

The earth is black now. The blue and orange light in the deepening night radiates softly around them.

The two remaining delinquents finish putting everything into the black plastic bags and tell the four they're nothing but dirty Indians and why the fuck do you come to Mexico from your backwaters? We'll slice you up when we're done with you, cut off your little cocks and balls and feed them to our dogs and chickens, they laugh.

The darkness rises in the sky and begins to close on their

prone bodies. Emilio can dimly see the blood dripping onto the dirt from Jonatan's wound. The one with a gun orders them to spread their legs and the other goes man to man and sticks his index and middle fingers roughly into their assholes looking for more money. He doesn't find anything and disappointed and angry, he now kicks them in their sides or legs and tells them how when the others return they are really going to get fucked. The four lie on the dark earth, silent and terrified, and without volition Emilio pisses himself. The warm liquid pools softly on the dirt beneath him, wets his thighs and lower belly, and the wire in his body strongly holds him in a stiff taut line. The winch behind his chest cranks tighter. His ribs ache and his feet burn, his anus.

One of the delinquents smells the urine, it is an acrid concentrated odor after the long day in the sun and his limited water intake, and says, Son of a fucking bitch, son of the great whore, one of you pissed yourself. Who did it?

Silence, but for the rising noise of the insect cacophony in the brush in the oncoming night.

I said *who*, motherfuckers.

The other delinquent laughs and says it's going to be worse for all of you if someone doesn't confess.

Me.

You? What's your name, faggot?

. . .

I said what's your name?

Emilio.

Listen to me, Emilio: you're nothing but a little piece of shit, he says, and kicks him several times in his side. He and the other young delinquent laugh uproariously.

The three others return and the leader with the gun says come on, lets go. They gather up the large bags and before they run off tell them they'd better not move.

The four lie still until they can no longer hear movement in the brush, and then Pedro lifts his head. He whispers that they have gone and stands and Jonatan and Emilio and William follow his lead.

They are naked and dirty and Jonatan's face and neck has blood covering it.

Emilio, by some small miracle, sees the small shining white stone and goes over and picks it up and presses his hand around it.

Mother of Jesus, Pedro says. Mother of God.

The men walk in the direction the three delinquents took Matilde on the small dirt path, afraid to call out her name and of what they will find. They see her body one hundred yards away in a small clearing at the base of a tree in the remaining light of the crepuscule. The branches above her head are covered with bright hanging cloth and look for a moment to the men's eyes like an evergreen trimmed for the Christmas season. As the men near the girl, however, they realize that in reality the colorful ornaments are dozens of pairs of women's underwear and brassieres. Matilde lies prone and naked beneath the wild canopy and Emilio thinks for a moment she might be dead. Then he hears her low cries, he sees her body shaking, and he is relieved, thank God, thank God, he thinks.

Pedro kneels down and gently lifts her up and says let's go, hurry, we are not too far from a settlement.

Emilio follows behind Pedro, who supports most of Matilde's weight with one of his arms around her waist. They move as fast as they can in their bare feet. Matilde whimpers softly and bleeds from her sex, blood has streaked down her legs, and Emilio thinks he can see teeth marks on one of her shoulders. When Pedro tires Emilio says that he can carry her now. He puts the white stone inside his mouth and lifts her up in his arms and she continues weeping softly. He follows Pedro and feels her blood wet the skin of his hip and his body is on a wire.

The naked party of five move through the night, vulnerable and afraid. The only thing Emilio now carries on this earth is the white California stone inside his mouth and the girl in his arms.

They see a light and a small shack in the distance behind a wire fence. They can hear dogs barking. The group ducks underneath the fence and approaches the house and Pedro knocks at the door.

We have a lady here who is hurt, Pedro says. We were assaulted in the hills.

Go away, the voice says, get out of here.

The five walk on.

Jonatan takes Matilde from Emilio's arms when Emilio can no longer carry her. They knock on another door behind another fence and are told to leave and a third.

They afterward see a small dark cornfield and beyond it a modest house with a light illuminated inside. An invisible dog begins barking loudly.

Please, we have a lady, and she is hurt. We are poor. We were assaulted in the hills.

An older woman opens the front door a small crack and sees Matilde, naked and crying in Jonatan's embrace. She sees the open cut on Jonatan's face and the other three behind them: dirty, naked, and terrified.

Mother of God, she says, why do you Central Americans do this to yourselves?

She calls her husband, who comes in from another room, and he takes a look at them and without saying anything leads them to a lean-to behind the main house. It is three concrete walls and corrugated aluminum for a roof and plastic sheeting for a fourth wall and door; a dirt floor. There is a bare light bulb suspended on a wire. The man switches the light on and they see several large plastic bags of what smell like fertilizer stacked against one of the concrete walls.

Stay here, the man says.

May God bless you, Pedro says.

Jonatan helps Matilde lie down on the ground and she curls into a fetal position with her back to the men. The men don't look at one another or at her; they squat down on the dirt in an attempt at modesty and wait. Emilio removes the white stone from his mouth and stares at it and thinks he sees her blood mixed with the dark earth deep inside the lines of his palm.

The old man brings two blankets and old trousers and old tee shirts for the men; he has a woman's shirt and skirt for Matilde. He says that he doesn't have shoes for them but he will tell them tomorrow where they might procure some. Pedro covers Matilde with the blanket and she holds it to herself tightly.

The men dress quickly in the trousers, happy to have something to cover themselves with, and soon the farmer's wife brings two plastic buckets of water, two clean rags, and a piece of soap.

This water is for her to clean up, she says, and she nods her head toward Matilde, who lies next to the bags of fertilizer, and for his face, she says to Jonatan. The second bucket is for you to drink. I'll bring you something to eat.

Pedro asks Matilde if he can help her sit up, but she doesn't respond. The men drink a little water and then Pedro says there are some clothes for you, we'll turn our backs. Drink some water, he says.

The four turn away and eventually they hear the girl moving around. The rag is wetted, and they hear her washing herself and dressing.

After she is finished she wraps the blanket around her body again despite the heat in the small lean-to, and lies down on the dirt with her back to the men.

Pedro examines Jonatan's cut and says fortunately it doesn't look too deep. Jonatan says he is fine and remains uncharacteristically quiet while Pedro tends it. The four men sit on their haunches and wait in silence for the señora to return. The invisible dog has begun barking once more outside the walls of the lean-to.

The señora brings tortillas and refried beans and a half-filled liter bottle of orange soda. This is all we can give you, she says, we don't have much, and you can't stay long. It's dangerous for us to keep you here. She leaves again through the plastic sheeting.

We should eat, Pedro says into their continuing silence and over the sounds of the insects from the cornfields and the dog's intermittent barking.

I don't want food, Emilio thinks, I don't want any of this. Not this night or day. He drinks a little of the orange soda at Pedro's insistence and each of them, except for Matilde, takes a tortilla and wraps some beans in it because Pedro says that they must keep up their strength. She has not moved again or spoken.

At least drink a little soda, Pedro says to her back. Matilde, you have to drink something and you should try to eat.

Matilde turns over and they don't look at her directly. They are chewing and quiet and staring at the dirt or at the concrete walls or the plastic bags of fertilizer behind her or the plastic sheeting. Emilio is thinking, I feel sick but I am eating and I don't want this but I have had it and it has sickened something inside me.

Matilde sits up and picks up a tortilla and opens her mouth, but she doesn't put it inside. She places the tortilla back onto the plate and instead drinks a sip of sweet orange soda and begins to gag. She vomits until nothing else will come up and dry heaves for a time, only yellow mucus and orange spittle dribble from her mouth. Pedro quietly holds her hair back from her face as she retches onto the dirt, saying, girl, girl, you'll be all right, you are okay now, muchacha. She continues to cry softly and all four men feel sick at heart and frightened and ashamed. Jonatan cleans up the vomit with one of the rags while Pedro eases her back down onto her side and continues to speak to her gently underneath his breath. The lean-to smells of their sweat and fear and her sour effluent and the ammonia from the fertilizer, but they are thankful for the concrete walls and the clothes they wear and the one light—all tangible barriers to the night.

You have to leave early in the morning, the old man says when he returns to see if they need anything else. We could get into trouble, my wife and me.

Thank you, señor.

It is the first act of mercy in Mexico and they are grateful for it.

Suck it, the man said. The man was shoving his gun into his mouth and threatening him. She was beside him and naked and beautiful and he also had the desire to fuck her but his terror was taking hold of him and squeezing his throat and he thought he would swallow the gun and its magazine, or the man would squeeze the trigger and his brain matter would fly into the atmosphere and travel thousands of miles from southern North America northward until his mother could apprehend him from his flesh in the nave at St. Joseph's.

In their living room in Berkeley. The hundred-year-old coast live oak had disappeared from the view of the bay window. He walked into the kitchen and his mother was standing at the stove preparing a soup. His sisters were sitting at the table and they were eating black rice and drinking black milk. Where has the tree gone? Brenda looked up at him in surprise. Dad cut it down, she said. He was certain that it had died already.

The señora brings them black coffee and sweet rolls at dawn. She gives them a large plastic bottle filled with lemonade to take with them.

Go with God, she says.

Her husband directs them to a safe house where they can procure shoes and where you can recover, he says.

The men walk one on each side and one in front of and behind Matilde on the dirt road. She walks slowly, tentatively. It still hurts me, she says.

In under two hours, the sun pushing onto the tops of their heads, the air humid and thick, sweaty and exhausted again, they arrive in Tapachula. Pedro asks directions to the street where the refuge is located and they make their way, shoeless and weary.

The five write their names in the house's ledger once they have been let inside the building. Pedro tells a volunteer about their troubles yesterday and she says she is hearing so many terrible things now, brother, you should consider returning to your country.

They bathe and receive clean clothes and they feel safe and clean and for today their worries lie on the other side of the high concrete walls of this House of the Migrants. The volunteers give them salve for their injuries and Emilio rubs the white greasy emollient on the soles of his feet and on the red sores on his toes and on his swollen ankles. He hopes the ladies in the privacy of the medical room tended Matilde's wounds and gave her pain medication; she did at least look more comfortable afterward, he thinks. A volunteer nurse gave Jonatan eleven small stitches and there is now a long red line crisscrossed by black cotton sutures on his cheek. Many of the migrants walk around in borrowed plastic sandals inside the house to let their feet heal and dry in the air. Emilio stays off his feet because each step is still painful.

We'll stay two nights, Pedro says to them. He knows Matilde needs to rest and recover some before they move on.

The next morning Emilio plays rummy with William and Jonatan to pass the time after breakfast. He wins three games in a row and Jonatan jokes that he can tell Emilio was educated by gringos because like them he tries to beat Latin Americans at every turn. Why are the yanquis so cold-hearted? he says to lighten the mood.

Before lunch is served the father of the refuge gives a talk about the dangers of the train and the crossing and how they ought to consider returning to their countries because Chiapas is not safe for them. Spicy bean soup with corn tortillas and chicken is then provided. There is sweet punch to drink and it is purple and ice-cold in the middle of the heat of the day upon the house. Emilio drinks it eagerly, realizing that already he is very different from the person of three days ago who worried about ice made with unfiltered water.

When he's finished eating, Pedro says he is going to town with a volunteer to pick up the wire. His cousin in Arizona promised to send a hundred dollars last night after Pedro had phoned and told him of their troubles on the road.

We shouldn't carry too much cash going forward.

I'll repay you when we reach Mexico City, Emilio told him.

We'll sort it out there, Pedro said.

Emilio now sits outside in a plastic chair beneath an old metal awning next to Matilde. She looks better than yesterday, less exhausted, and she is sewing buttons on men's shirts and fixing torn collars and holes in the fabric to be of some assistance to the shelter. A pile of donated clothing in need of repair sits in a large box at her side. It is hot and the air is thick and he is drowsy in the heat because his belly is filled from lunch and the four glasses of sugary punch he drank and because he has not slept well in days. She sews competently; she is experienced and sure about it, she bites the cotton thread strongly and the needle flies through cloth and he can see that this normal activity is a balm for her.

Thick white clouds gather in small groups in the bright blue sky above them. He and the girl are shielded from the sun's harshest rays by the overhang, but he sweats through his shirt quickly in the relentless heat and humidity. Tomorrow morning looms in front of them and he waits for it to arrive, he is antsy to continue, he is afraid, but this progressive force is still upon him and he knows he must keep going, checks the pocket of the jeans he is wearing, feels for the white stone and fingers it. I still have it, he thinks, that is something, and I am with them, with her. He looks closely at Matilde and she looks different, still very pretty, her dark hair long and clean down her back, her face scrubbed and new clothes which fit her better, but there is a change he can see in the deep lines that have formed on each side of her mouth, as if something about her pulls inwardly now, her face, her shoulders, the two protruding bars of her clavicles. Matilde, maybe you should go back, he says into the silence and thick air between them.

The words moved out of his mouth as if of their own volition toward the blue cloth in her hands, surprising even him.

She doesn't look up from her work. She concentrates on her sewing, pulls the needle through cloth several more times.

With nothing to show for my efforts? she finally says.

But at least you'll be safe.

She makes another stitch.

You ought to consider it.

Emilio, she eventually says.

You ought to—

He sees more clouds gathering whitely and moving across the liquid sky as she mends the blue shirt. Sweat drips down the sides of his face and down the center of his back.

We'll make it, she says.

She doesn't look at him, only downward at the work in her lap.

The worst has happened now.

He looks at the slight girl who is efficient in her sewing and lovely beside him, her shoulders slightly rounded as if she wished to fold unto herself.

I can figure out a way to get you money if you need some money, he says.

Please stop saying it.

I don't understand . . . why?

She is quiet again and he looks up at the white clouds again. There are stars I cannot see behind the light of the day, he thinks.

After several more minutes have passed, still concentrating on the blue shirt, she says his name once more and then (her voice when she speaks is quiet and subdued, lacking in meanness or spite): I knew of the risks before I left my country.

He watches her as she now takes another shirt from the box, examines it, and once she discovers the tear at the seam of the collar begins to mend it.

But it's not safe for you, probably for any woman crossing Mexico. I understand that now.

She doesn't reply, pulls more thread from the spool in her lap, and he worries he has angered this girl he hardly knows and yet toward whom he feels inexplicably drawn, as if he is inside a magnetic field when she is near him.

She concentrates on her task. She sews. He is hotter, there is no breeze to cool him; the air is heavy and humid and his stomach is still very full and his eyelids involuntarily begin to droop; he sweats; he thinks he might fall asleep. He leans farther back in the plastic chair and closes his eyes. He wishes the wind would lift and cool him and he thinks of the cold water of the Pacific Ocean at home and of the immense freshwater lake three hours north in the Sierra Nevada mountains. And then, as if from below the surface of the blue water, he hears her voice again, lacking meanness or spite, when she says his name a third time.

I still have my dream and that's all that I have now, the voice continues. There is no work in my country, or the job ends, or the war tax is half your wages and not enough remains to cover the most basic expenses, or the day arrives when they come after you and your family. The money runs out and the child is hungry and how will we pay his school fees next year? (Emilio opens his eyes and the bright white light of the day slams against him.) In my country (the story unspools like the cotton thread) we have no hope, only trouble: money troubles, gang troubles, troubles with the government, corruption, and the violence. Two years ago when they killed my husband (Emilio sits up straight in the plastic chair and he looks at her sharply. She continues to speak deliberately into the stationary air as if without volition and now without surcease.) I didn't know why or who and if you ask questions you have even more problems because the police are like the criminals, same as those two cops who beat you, and no different from the delinquents yesterday. So I had to shut up and we buried him. There was no police investigation because the police never carry out investigations in Tegucigalpa.

Matilde, he says.

Two men rode by him on a motorbike and one shot him in the head. Some people whispered it was because he was working with the gang in the colonia, but that was a lie. He was an electrician and he was just twenty-three when they got him. He was on his way to the corner store to buy rice, bread, and milk. It was simply bad luck. Tegus became worse three years ago when the army took out the elected president (She pauses. Wipes both sides of her face, and then resumes her stitching) and I moved in with my mother and younger sister after that, but there is never enough money and so I do it for them. I have two: a boy who is four, and a girl who is one year behind him.

The blue liquid above him, the altering white forms, the heat, and this woman with the moving hands and quiet unspiteful voice.

I didn't know you had two children, I didn't know you were married, you look so young and you . . . I didn't know about the problems in Honduras, he says.

She pulls the needle through the last edge of the tear on the collar and closes it.

I'm twenty-two (she finds and begins to mend a third shirt. Her hands move and her voice is an accompanying machine), not so young. But when there is no man in the house some people get ideas and my father has been gone for many years. Two months ago a guy in our neighborhood started talking to my sister as she walked home from school and he began calling the house all the time and she was afraid. I moved her across town to live with Pedro and my stepsister, Ana, in another neighborhood and to another school, but it's not secure there either because one or the other gang control that colonia also. They can find you anywhere. They have checkpoints; they watch who comes, who goes. So we live shut inside our houses with metal bars on the windows and doors.

She pauses. He watches her and he waits. He listens.

In Honduras there is no future for us. No hope. I want something better for my children, for my sister, and so all of this, it's nothing. (She is still pushing the needle into the third shirt, mending another tear in the fabric, not looking at him, only speaking into the day between them in this strange and hallowed voice.) I was warned about the dangers on the journey and I took the necessary precautions.

He watches the needle piercing the cloth.

Another pause in her speech. The unstopping work of her hands.

I will get there (the southern sky of Mexico above him, above all of them at this shelter, the hands and cloth and the voice of the faithful, her turned-in visage), God willing, she says.

And she has been crying while she speaks, but she doesn't look away from her task (or at him), only at the jagged holes, the cotton thread, the mending. She uses her teeth on the thread again and ties a knot, and her left hand lifts and wipes her eyes and across her cheeks as it has many times already when she can no longer see the work in her lap from the tears clouding her vision. Her large dark-brown eyes darkened, the needle pushed and pulled, her left hand lifted to wipe her cheeks again and again; the two new lines around her mouth held her lips together carefully.

Okay, he says.

She is dressed in blue jeans and a white tee shirt which advertises an American beer company. She is looking at the work in her lap and the voice has quieted, gone back into itself. He watches her and he knows suddenly and irrationally that he wants to protect her from further travails. She is beautiful, he thinks, even now and under these circumstances, something emanates from her. I don't understand it, but I can see.

I want to help you, he says.

The next morning they walk into Bombilla. Hundreds of migrants sit on the train tracks and on the dirt and talk and wait and worry another humid hot day. Some women and a few children and teenagers mingle among the crowd, but Bombilla is predominantly filled with men in baseball caps and worn-out shoes with small day packs slung across their shoulders. Their sunburnt faces. A look of fear and insecurity resides inside their half-lidded eyes for the days that lie ahead, unknown and chaotic. Some migrants say they have been waiting for the train for four days; a Salvadoran they speak to says he's been here for three but he hopes one will arrive shortly. The trains do not run on any predictable schedule in the south.

The five find a spot alongside the rails and sit down. Vendors walk the tracks and sell their wares: sandwiches, potato chips, bottles of water, Coke, Fanta, cookies, and frozen fruit popsicles. Around noon, Jonatan buys a liter of soda from a young boy, and then some tortillas and refried beans from a transvestite who smiles at him when she takes his pesos and says, What happened to your face, gorgeous, you okay now?

The five share the repast.

The men keep an eye out for the police in black uniforms in case there is a need to run, but the air is thick and the sky is hazy and the afternoon goes by slowly. They are bored, they are anxious. If I had my book now I would read it, Emilio thinks, if I had my journal and pen I might write what I've seen, the miles I've traveled.

When she comes we need to be ready, Pedro says. And he tells them again how to board the Beast, how she will have no pity, to never hesitate when boarding a moving train. Grab the ladder and hold on with both hands, don't let go, he says to Matilde for the third or fourth time, or you risk getting pulled beneath the wheels.

They wait all day in the sunshine and at dusk the heat slowly relaxes on their bodies. Darkness begins to fall on the yard and black shadows and the unlighted corridors lift into the night as the half-dozen dim streetlamps of Bombilla turn on. Night in Chiapas is the terror it brings, wall-less and open. The stars begin to illumine the heavens above them, copious and bright.

When will it arrive, she asks. And she asks the question without expecting an answer for she has asked it many times already. The men keep an eye on the tracks and on the deep shadows; they watch for any movements in the night. The girl twists her hair around her index and middle fingers continuously.

The low melancholy whistle of a train sounds in the distance. Emilio turns his left wrist to see the time and remembers again that his watch is no longer on his arm. It could be three a.m., he thinks. They are fortunate because they have only waited eighteen hours.

The mob of people at the depot stand and move nearer to the tracks. The horn blows again and an orb of light approaches along the night corridor. Someone is yelling this is it, grab this one, as the enormous engine drives into the depot. The five walk with Matilde between them and then they are running when Pedro says go!, and he is telling her to run faster and grab it first, and she reaches out her right arm and takes hold of the metal ladder attached to the outside of a boxcar. She is terrified of slipping and Pedro is yelling at her to get it with both hands and to pull hard, put your inside foot on the ladder first and don't let go, whatever you do, Matilde, do not let the metal rung go for any reason. She places her foot on the ladder and another migrant already aboard the train helps her up, saying, this way, señorita, come on come on, and then she is standing on the metal landing area at the end of a hopper. Emilio sees her smile flash brightly with her straight white teeth, and one by one they begin to jump up behind her. Emilio's heart is pounding furiously in his chest as he tries to recall all the things Pedro has told him and he is the second-to-last to board, he smiles at her in the dimness as soon as he is on the hopper; she leans against him slightly and he shivers in the warm night. Pedro jumps up last, and they are all relieved to have boarded with relative ease and contented to be on a moving train. Migrants cover most of the surface area of the cargo train: its roofs and ends and ladders. No one rides inside, however: all of the boxcars are locked to the night.

Have you ever been able to ride inside one of the containers? Emilio had asked Pedro earlier in the day.

Sometimes you can find an open car and then you just have to make sure you don't get locked inside. Fifteen years ago, when I first took the Beast it was easy: there was less crime and the train attendants would often, for a little bite, maybe fifty pesos, open the doors so we could all ride inside comfortably. But those days are over, muchacho. Now we sit on top or at the ends of cars, sometimes if we are fortunate we can ride in an open car on the top of lumber or piles of coal.

The five of them make their way to the top of the crowded boxcar and find a place to sit together. The train begins to pick up speed. With the increasing wind and movement, they begin to feel lighthearted. The loud whistle blows, the engine rumbles and clanks, and the train cars move laterally in the night air as the Beast lurches ahead. We are finally going, Emilio thinks.

The waxing moon is nearly half-full above their heads. They pass through small towns and across dark fields, then through more small towns, and because Emilio has always lived in a city he has rarely seen the canopy of the heavens open out as densely as it does tonight in the countryside. He notices the North Star sits lower in the sky in southern Mexico than at home.

Even Matilde looks a little more relaxed, he thinks, when he glances at her from time to time as they pass through a town. She leans toward him now and again. But even when she is not beside him, he senses her. He has begun to track her movements involuntarily with his eyes, with his body.

She was standing by the tracks and it was night. An electric streetlamp lifted shadows from the ground, the shanties, the stationary train cars. He saw her and he said her name. She turned when he called to her and he didn't recognize her, although she was herself, but his eyes, for some reason, could not apprehend her.

Antonia, he said again.

Soon he was holding her and pressing the slim torso, the light-brown hair and small breasts, against his body. He was kissing the brown lips of the girl and he was aroused and she loved him back, she kissed him deeply, and then she stepped away from him and pressed the thumb, index, and middle fingers of her right hand together to form a circle and the other two fingers pointed skyward. This was the benediction, he knew. Mamá, he said, and peered into her face closely, tried to see clearly, and her visage then sharply emerged as if he were looking at a photograph. Matilde was smiling the beatific smile of repose and the promise of the relief of his suffering, as in an old religious icon. And he felt it then, a loosening in his tightened chest and bowels, like birds rushing out from a copse.

By morning they are all exhausted. No one has slept for more than a half hour at a time and some of the thrill of speed and progress has waned with their fatigue. Emilio's ribs ache, and he thinks that Jonatan's face looks drawn, his wound looks pinched around the stitches. Matilde is sitting next to Jonatan with the hood of the grey sweatshirt they gave her at the shelter pulled tightly around her head so that he can't see her eyes.

When the train stops we'll get off to find some food and then pick up the next one, Pedro says. We don't want to hang around Chiapas too long, too many problems for us in this state.

Emilio thinks how he is not certain what he would do without Pedro's guidance and assurances, he himself cannot say which route the train follows, which towns are good to stop in, which are not.

As the train pulls into the next depot they jump off and go search for a place to relieve themselves. They find a makeshift bathroom area, and although it is dirty and fly-filled and smells of shit and urine, it is better than the open air or bushes or pissing off the back of the moving train, especially for Matilde. Afterward they fill their bottles from a spigot at the side of the tracks and drink deeply and then buy two tacos each from a vendor. Within minutes of finishing their food, they hear the wail of another train horn and Pedro says it's time to go. The five run back to the tracks and scramble aboard.

There's enough space below at the end of this hopper for two of them to sit where it's shaded and more comfortable and Jonatan, they decide, will stay down with Matilde. The other three climb to the roof of the adjacent graffiti-covered boxcar.

The day goes and the metal of the car heats up and red blisters begin to form on Emilio's hands where he holds the metal grating beneath him. He knows he must hold on tightly at the moments when the train lurches or suddenly picks up speed or risk falling. The boxcars of this fifteen-car train are covered over with migrants and the dry land, the green trees, the dirt roads, and the small towns go by them. He is dozing on the flat hot metal grate when the train slows in another small town and two dozen more migrants jump aboard. Pedro whispers to him to remember how they can't trust everyone, some of the Salvadorans and even the Hondurans might work for the gangs or cartels as falcons, he says. They sit in their group of three and watch the tilled fields and telephone poles and wires and wide sky and fall asleep for five and ten minutes at a time. The sun is at its zenith and Emilio is hot and tired and thirsty and although they have half a bottle of water remaining, they are rationing it since they don't know when they'll next be able to fill their bottles, or when they will secure more food.

The enormous train picks up speed and travels faster now. The trees spread out to the left and right of the tracks and cover the land, and it seems to Emilio suddenly that he is flying through space, as if he were on a ride at an amusement park, gliding across the tree tops, over the wide green earth, into the blue sky and yellow-white sunlight. The wind is pushing the black soot from his face and teeth and he feels again the exhilaration he felt for the first time yesterday. The beauty of the land in relief against his own sharp aliveness and the speed of the train fill him wildly. I'll make it, he thinks. I'm young and strong and smart and I'm returning to the place where I belong. He looks at his left wrist and the lighter-colored band on his arm is sunburnt and becoming the same dark brown as the rest of his arm and he wonders what time it is and if his mom is still at work at the bakery, if Brenda has come home from school yet, which class Antonia might be attending today. Is it cold and fog-covered in Berkeley? And then he wonders if Matilde is sleeping down below, what she's thinking about, how she's feeling. If she, like him, is thinking about her family: her children, her sister, and mother. But why am I thinking about her? he thinks. And how is it that despite my circumstances I feel a sensation of freedom at this moment as I travel across the earth's surface on the top of this massive loud old locomotive that I haven't known before? I'm not sure anymore what is a dream or nightmare and what is real, but speed does it, he thinks, the verdant land they pass through, and the Beast, the progress it makes, the unexpected expansion of spirit it caused.

The noise from the train never abates, all day and into the night: it is loud and cranks and keeps its noise on the tops of their ears. Emilio holds onto the metal gridwork in the dark. It must be four in the morning or thereabouts and cold and black before him. He pulls the sweater he is wearing close to his body. He can't see the faces of the men and the few women and doesn't trust anyone he doesn't know and sometimes the engineer brakes the train and slows it down, and then it speeds up again through the night. Jonatan and Pedro are by his side and William is below with Matilde. I've known them less than a week, which under normal circumstances is hardly any time at all, he thinks, but these are not normal circumstances and they have become indispensable companions and my friends.

Emilio is covered in the carbon that covers the tracks and it irritates his nose and eyes. He is black like the night and the faces he can't see seem at moments to move across his retinae. He and Pedro and Jonatan take turns helping one another to stay awake and vigilant against the unknown. Their eyelids shutter and they shake themselves. We must do our best, Pedro says, the Beast can be a killer in the dark. The stars push down on them, the train careens over the land. When they pass through a town the electric lights illuminate their bodies for a moment.

Some of the men on the tops of the hoppers and boxcars sing popular ballads during the long night to keep from falling asleep and to entertain themselves. Emilio catches snippets of the melodies as they move onto the air. Those that have belts tie

87

themselves to the metal grating of the train and close their eyes and sleep. Some use ropes to secure themselves. He can hear others speaking their prayers from time to time.

The light begins to augment in the sky and there are lighter blues and eventually yellows and the dark land assumes its forms on the fast-moving northbound train. Emilio can once again see the faces of his companions and he no longer worries that the Salvadoran at the front of the wagon with a tattoo on his neck of *Stefanie* in cursive writing is a gang falcon who might rob him or toss him from the car. The man laughs congenially with his companions. The light brings ease to the travelers on the train. Seeing is its own comfort, Emilio thinks.

Not long after sunrise, the train comes to a full stop in the middle of a large sugarcane field. For a moment there is panic among the travelers. Most of the men stand up to look out for the police or the migra or the army or delinquents, but after twenty minutes pass and nothing happens, everyone sits down and relaxes and several of the men jump off the train and cut down stalks of cane with small pocketknives. Pedro and Jonatan climb down the ladder with two other migrants, including the Salvadoran with the tattoo, and cut several stalks and rush back to the boxcar. Moments later the train lurches and begins moving again. Several migrants still in the field abandon their cuttings and run and jump back on.

Emilio joins the four at the end of the hopper and happily sucks from the long piece of cane Pedro has handed to him. They all enjoy the sweet juice tucked inside the plant's fibers as their breakfast this morning. Emilio begins to feel more energetic than he had only moments ago.

The most important thing is to give it our best, Pedro says.

After they finish their meal, Emilio stands with Matilde at the end of the hopper, they lean onto the metal railing and the wind rushes on them. She looks tired, but always lovely, he thinks.

Rest here for a few hours, Emilio, Pedro tells him, and the other three climb back up to the top of the boxcar.

He and the girl sit down and watch the fields pass them, the caravans of trees, and the distant hills. The train approaches another small town and the air horn wails three times. Emilio is contented to sit next to Matilde in the shade of the car and not ride above in the burning sunshine as the day heats up. She has pulled the hood of the sweatshirt off her head and twists her hair around the index finger of her left hand as she so often does. They watch the land and she is quiet and he is tired and quiet also.

I hope we can see each other again once we are in the North, she says.

He is surprised by her comment after the long silence but happy to hear it and says that he wishes to see her again also. He puts his hand into his pocket and finds the stone from home and rubs the pad of his thumb across it.

I hope you will come visit me wherever I stay and we can have a meal and afterward we can watch a television show, something relaxing, she continues. I know it's stupid, but that's what I want to do. I want to spend a lazy day with you and Pedro and Jonatan and William eating a good meal, drinking cold beers, watching TV. I'll make you a baleada!

That would be nice, he says. Or you can visit me in Berkeley and we'll watch the cold fog creep across the bay in a white-grey sheet from the Golden Gate Bridge to my house to cover the hills behind it.

Isn't California sunny and warm?

Where I grew up on the northern coast it is frequently over-cast and grey, especially in summer.

It's cold in the summer? Then I guess you'll have to come visit me in Arizona.

Yes, I can do that.

Is it true what everyone says?

Says about what?

That all the jobs pay at least eight dollars per hour. That it's modern. Safe. And women are treated better, life is better there.

He looks at her while she is talking and perhaps he is even miss-ing some of her words or putting others in their place over and under the loud grinding of the Beast's metal wheels against the rails. And he feels a sensation in his stomach, but not the winch that is constant and his fears, something else: when he looks at this slim girl he sees again that small bright thing that emanates from her no matter the heat and dark nights and wind and noise and insects and hunger and thirst. Perhaps it is her hopefulness. Chiapas goes by them and he sits with the Honduran girl he found by chance and about whom, he finds, he cannot stop thinking.

You are beautiful, he says in English.

What did you say?

It's nothing, he says, and soon falls asleep. His head is against her shoulder and the movement of the train rocks him and jolts him awake occasionally. He is not dreaming. Then he dreams of the train noise, a small town, a large metropolis, and of her. Of the towns they pass through and the señoras walking alongside the train tracks with large colorful plastic bowls of corn masa on their heads that they will later use to make tortillas for their families.

He was driving across the Richmond Bridge even though he was not a driver. He had left Berkeley behind, and he was heading toward Marin County and the sea. The enormous cantilever bridge leaned in closely to his car with its steel trusses and he worried that he would lose control of the vehicle and fall down into the cold bay waters below him. I am going to Muir Beach and it's the most beautiful one, isn't it? he said to the girl next to him in the passenger seat.

. . .

Bridges have always terrified me, he said.
You must remember, God is in everything.
In you?

He jerks awake and sees Matilde lying with her head resting on his thigh. Her face is relaxed and calm and her wide lips are slightly parted and as he gazes at her he thinks again how pretty she is and he knows this attraction is not right because of Antonia in Berkeley, because of everything, but he feels it nonetheless.

Pedro climbs down the ladder and tells him he's very tired and would he mind if he takes his spot for a few hours? She wakes up briefly when Emilio moves his legs and Pedro sits down in his place and she goes back to sleep. Emilio climbs to the top of the moving train; he is still tired and his eyes sting. He walks carefully on the metal grates to maintain his balance on the train's roof as he looks for Jonatan and William and finds them toward the front of the boxcar. William lies on his back in the middle of the car where there is no metal grate and it's more comfortable. He is quiet as always, and Jonatan is talking animatedly to another traveler. It must be the middle of the day now, Emilio thinks as he sits down next to them, the sun strong above them, the sky hazy and bright.

Jonatan introduces the tall gangly man as Royo.

It's the kid's first time on the Beast, Jonatan continues. They sent him back a few weeks ago.

Welcome to the Train of Death my friend, Royo says, and he smiles congenially.

Emilio notices the dirty jeans hanging off the bones of the man's skinny legs, the old tee shirt that swings loosely around his torso and wiry dark arms. Have you ridden her before? he asks.

This is my third time. The first was back in ninety-seven, and in two thousand three I returned home when my mother was dying.

How has it been?

We go because we have to, right?

Emilio says yes and looks at the dry trees covering the landscape, at the dirt and afternoon sky and green weeds and rolling hills while the swaying motion of the Beast lulls him. He sees dozens of men and women sitting and lying on the tops of the boxcars far out in front of him—baseball capped or heads wrapped in old tee shirts to protect against the sun. Some sit staring out at the countryside as he does, many doze, and he also wants to close his eyes again and sleep despite the hours below next to Matilde. He thinks of her lying against Pedro's body, her face now pressed to his thigh.

Time for a little siesta, Jonatan says, and stretches out next to William. Blood has coagulated along the taut line of stitches on his face and makes a strange grimace on his left cheek.

What's taking you north this time? Emilio asks Royo.

Mine are all up there, Royo says, with a small lift of his chin, so I have to go. But you should have a care, especially this first time. I once saw a young inexperienced kid get fucked.

What happened? Emilio asks.

It was in Veracruz and the kid was trying to board in one of the small towns. He was running and reached his hand up for the ladder and the men on board were encouraging him, yelling get it kid, get it, but the boy, you know, maybe he was twelve or thirteen years old, he grabbed for it and then he changed his mind because he got scared or he couldn't manage it and by then all of us on the train were screaming hold on, hold on, muchacho, don't let go, put both your feet on the ladder! The men closest to him at the end of a hopper tried to grab his arms but the kid wasn't resolute or he wasn't strong enough to maintain his grip and then it was too late and the Beast dragged him down underneath her. We saw the bottom half of the kid's body fly onto the dirt, his legs in blue jeans and still wearing old tennis shoes. But the Beast just kept rolling forward, picking up speed, and we left him there. I'd seen some things like that before, when a man is careless and lost a foot or an arm, but he was a child, you know? Not much older than my oldest boy is now, and it was terrible to see him get fucked like that.

Emilio closes his eyes for a moment against the hazy strong sunshine and Royo's story and his torso begins to sway radically. He feels a hand on his shoulder and he slams his eyes back open to the train and to Chiapas moving by them and the men all around him. He grabs for the metal grate beneath his legs.

My advice to you, kid, is to hold on tightly, even if she seems to be moving along quietly and calmly, as she is now, and you're sitting close to the edge. If the migra comes, run for your life. And if the train stops in the middle of nowhere, jump off and run into the jungle because delinquents or narcos or the police are going to board it. Run into the wilderness if you want to remain free.

As Emilio listens to Royo he feels nervous and afraid, but the movements of the train and the sunshine continue to lull him nonetheless. His eyes burn. I am so tired, he thinks, I want to sleep. I'm hungry. He gazes at the passing thin bedraggled trees, at a lone telephone pole with blackbirds sitting on it who lift into busy flight when the Beast roars by them. Royo opens a half-eaten bag of potato chips and following the laws of hospitality on the train offers some to Emilio. The chips are oily and salty and hurt the sore gums in Emilio's mouth as they mix with the thick saliva on his tongue and he is grateful for them. These are delicious, he says.

They sit quietly for a time and the sun beats down on their bodies unremittingly. Jonatan and William continue to doze at the center of the boxcar and Emilio holds onto the grate, fighting against his fatigue and hunger and watching the countryside as it moves by them.

Royo begins to sing:

> Mexico is beautiful
> But how I suffered the five thousand
> kilometers I traveled
> I can tell you that I remember each one.

Do you know it? he asks when he's finished and Emilio tells him that he doesn't.

Here's one I made up this trip:

> There are too many dangers on the road, O Lord
> How difficult the journey for migrants
> How long
> We put our faith in you, Señor
> Keep us in Your sight.

Do you sing in your church, kid?

Emilio shakes his head no.

It's good to sing riding atop the Beast: it keeps you awake and it keeps up the spirit. I discovered its benefits when I went north. I was in Houston at first without my señora and the kids, you been there? Washing dishes at a Chinese and most people were decent and if I could make enough money to feed everyone at home and pay school fees then it was good. But it was lonely too. No one ever tells you that when they talk about the United States: how it's a lonely country. Was it like that for you?

Emilio shakes his head no again. He watches the trees, the next flock of blackbirds on the next telephone pole. He follows the line of an adjacent dirt road with his eyes until he can't see it any longer.

You were lucky then.

Yes.

Me, I got lonely without my family, Royo says. And all those beers they served extra cold at the local had my number! My señora insisted I attend service again, and once she joined me with the boys we all started singing together in our small choir.

Was it difficult to bring them? Emilio asks.

Eh muchacho, those were different times. Easier times. It used to be a man could come and work and then go, before the gringos shut the border up like a lock. And there was less delinquency on the road. Now if you're lucky enough to make it inside, you can't ever leave because it's gotten so difficult and expensive to get back in!

What changed?

Everything! Royo smiles. The coyotes started to charge more, and now they all are on the narcos' payroll. And once the narcos treated us like a business, like a commodity that can be sold for more money, then our problems got really bad. Traveling solo like I'm doing now has gotten complicated.

He smiles again.

I've been shaken down dozens of times over the years, by the police mostly, because the Mexican police are sons of bitches to Central Americans, that's how I got this scar on my forehead. Royo points to a scar between his eyes. But what the narcos are now doing is something else. Something of the Devil himself.

Still, mine have been waiting for me for eight months, ever since I got deported. I'm the breadwinner of my family. We go because we've got to get back to them, right?

Yes.

And Mexico *is* a beautiful country, don't you think? Royo gestures to the land and sky with his hand and bony arm.

Yes, Emilio says.

It's too bad it's filled with Mexicans!

They both laugh.

Look how many people cover the top of this long metal snake as she winds towards Oaxaca. See how a man will risk everything for his children and their future. Emilio sees all of the bodies sitting and lying across the surface of the boxcars that stretch out in front of and behind him, the hundreds of men and women, but not the unseeable reasons that propel them forward, northward.

Only God is our guide. I'll keep trying until I make it back to my kids. My third was born in Texas four years ago, so she's the first real gringa! And if you think about all this for a minute you will realize something: even our Lord Jesus Christ was a migrant at one time.

The day wanes and Emilio sees pack mules in the fields, white and blue pickup trucks in the small towns, a red jeep in the countryside, and near the tracks rows of humble storefronts and ramshackle houses. He is still hungry and thirsty and tired. His stomach rumbles continuously and he longs for a glass of cold water. He wishes he were like some of the people they pass who are walking home or to the store and the muleteer is coming in from the fields and everything is in the known world for them and orderly and dinner and a cold drink await them. We on this train are like modern nomads, he thinks, the uncharted before us, above us the Milky Way.

The Beast has picked up speed again. He is near the edge of the train car holding the grate tightly and his back and shoulders ache from gripping it, and more than anything he would like to sleep and this desire for sleep and its onslaught scares him more than the oncoming night. Give it your best, he is saying to himself inside of himself, echoing Pedro's constant refrain. His stomach rumbles again. His dry tongue is thick against the roof of his mouth.

The sun has finally set and the hot metal of the rooftops has begun to cool. The land and the forms of it darken: the mountains, the fields of corn and coffee, the shacks alongside them, the open plains and tall palm trees. Where the sun's orb disappears behind the mountains' edge, the red becomes orange then yellow as it fans out and rises into the blue, whiter to darker, higher in the sky. Emilio lies next to William now in the middle of the boxcar. Jonatan is on William's other side, and as Emilio stares up at the changing light he wonders when they'll get off the train, when they'll have a meal and something cold to drink. He thinks about what he would eat if he were at home: a large pizza from Sliver near Berkeley High and afterward something sweet, an ice cream from Ici. Or I'd go to the Chinese noodle place near campus and order two large bowls of hand-pulled noodles with beef. Maybe Mom has made chicken stew with rice for dinner tonight?

The gnawing in his stomach increases, the light darkens.

I need to stop thinking about food, he thinks, and he focuses his mind instead on the place itself: its streets, buildings, and shops (as if by imagining it it might again materialize). He sees the campus with its neoclassical architecture, its massive colonnades; he walks through Sather Gate toward the three-hundred-foot clock tower that is the city's landmark; he climbs the steps of Wheeler Hall where he took most of his classes. Then he sees Acme Bakery on San Pablo Boulevard where he worked the register on weekends for years, his mom shaping the sourdough baguettes in the back. The limestone fountain with the five kneeling bears in the roundabout at the base of Marin Avenue; Marin Avenue with its steep grade rising into the Berkeley Hills; the green hills in summer that catch the fog and hold it like a barricade. He sees the saltwater bay on the west edge of the city, Carleton Street, and his house near downtown. He sees his bedroom, the blue walls, his large comfortable bed and its grey coverlet. His mother is in the kitchen preparing a meal and Brenda sits at the dining table doing her homework. Susana will come over after she gets off work at Children's Hospital and perhaps she will sleep in her old bed tonight and not with Peter at their apartment. The lights are lighted, the doors are locked, if the fog rolled in, the heater has been turned on. Antonia will text him saying to come over once he's finished dinner. He sees it clearly: the city, his house, his mother and sisters, her. And he is thinking of the long distance between the top of this train, the last waning light of the crepuscule, the low-lying clouds, the wind steadily on him, Venus which emerged red-dotted in the sky only moments ago, and of his old life, his only life, in Berkeley. But perhaps I must not overly think about them or it, he thinks; there is only here, only now, only the Beast. I must stay alert, remain confident, pay attention: I will get there.

Inevitably on the heels of that thought another comes and his stomach tightens and fear pulls the wire stiffly up his throat.

What if I don't?

And then: Why are the people I love so far from me on the earth?

The night passes slowly. He lies on his belly and holds onto the metal grating and shivers from the cold. Royo is next to him. Watch out for the power lines ahead, a man in front of them yells down the train, and they hold their bodies closer and prone against the Beast's surface. Royo sings for a time and Emilio catches snippets of the song beneath the train's noise and horn-blowing. The Beast sways from side to side at intervals; most of the migrants quietly hold on.

What's it like where you grew up, Emilio eventually says into the dark to Royo to distract himself from the cold and his fatigue after Royo has stopped singing another ballad.

It's a pueblo called Rincón, Royo says close to his ear. To give you an idea of how remote and how small: I never had electricity until I moved to the United States, and for water we had a well fifteen minutes away on foot.

They are passing through a town now; its yellow lights soften the darkness. The horn blows three times to indicate their passage.

The people, however, are good, Royo continues. Each family with its plot of land and maize, plantains, beans, and everyone works hard and we maintain the traditional ways. There wasn't even a school nearby until I was a kid, so very few of the old generation learned to read.

The train has left the town behind and moved into darkness again. The stars are infinite and luminous above them, and several shoot across the sky, left to right and right to left, each time Emilio looks up.

My grandfather didn't know his letters, but he was renowned in my village, Royo says beneath the loud clankings of the train against the metal rails. He kept all the births and deaths, the marriages, the floods and fires, for generations. He could recite back to the beginnings, all the way to Adam when it was only pure Indians living there.

Low branches ahead, a voice ahead of them calls back. Watch out!

The men press their faces closer to the Beast's back in anticipation and soon the branches of trees begin to slap against their bodies. Emilio presses himself closely to the metal until his body is unhampered again and only wind again. The cosmos above.

Rincón is changing. Some families even have TVs now, Royo says, those who get remittances from their relatives in the north. Many have mobile telephones.

Small electric lights can be seen in the houses in the distance on each side of the loud train.

Everything changes, no? So we have to give it our best effort, Royo says. My baby girl, Yenny, loves to sing, just like her dad! And the boys speak English perfectly, but you must speak English perfectly too, no?

Yes, Emilio says, and thinks, I can't even recall my grandfather's full name, only the story my dad used to tell of how the soldiers came and took him in the middle of the night, how he never saw him again. But maybe this guy next to me is exaggerating about his grandfather? Still, I wonder if I were to concentrate, could I keep some of these stories in my mind for later? He closes his eyes for a moment as if to etch certain details into his memory and he begins to drift off, branches and leaves hit his spine and wake him and a few minutes later they quit once more. He looks up at the stars again and he lies on his bed on the grey coverlet and his mother is saying, Emilio did you break open your chicken bones and suck out their marrow?

Wake up, muchacho, or you will lose your grip, Royo says.

I think I'll go down below.

When they enter another town and Emilio can see with the light of the electric lamps, he gets up and carefully makes his way to the ladder and down to the end of the boxcar. He sees Matilde leaning against Pedro's body; they both appear to be sleeping. There are six others crammed in with them in the small space. He feels a surge of annoyance when he sees her leaning in so closely to Pedro's shoulder and he catches himself, asks himself what's wrong with me? He sits down and squeezes in next to Pedro and just before he falls asleep, cold and worried and hungry and thirsty, he thinks about Matilde, wishing she were nearer.

I am lost.

Two orange lions entered the room: a large male with a thick mane of orange fur like a halo around its head, and a smaller female. We'll have to kill the male and eat it, we're so hungry, a hunter dressed in military fatigues next to him announced. Then we'll hang its carcass on a wire.

I don't want to kill it, he said.

I have a bow and arrow you can use to shoot it. Afterward you'll be a real macho, the hunter said.

He looked closely at the two lions and noticed the male staring at him intently with its enormous amber eyes. The animal carefully followed his every move from behind the floor-to-ceiling plate glass that now separated them. Its massive orange head turned slowly from side to side as it tracked him.

I don't want to kill it, he said again.

Otherwise you will have nothing, the hunter said.

He is awake and looking out at the countryside, watching it transform. Pedro has gone to the top of the car to check on William and Jonatan, and Matilde sits to his right while another traveler, one of the other women on this car, dozes to his left. Matilde also stares off into the lightening green of the landscape. Dawn. He looks down at her and notices the bones in her jaw protrude more than they did one week ago: hunger has etched the bones more sharply. He knows that he too is losing weight, like all of them; Pedro's paunch is getting smaller every day.

Matilde looks up at him. She begins to twist her hair. Then she looks back at the passing land and after several minutes have passed, back again at him.

I keep wondering, she says close to his ear.

She lifts her hand to indicate the train, the fields.

Why are you doing this?

Why? Because I got deported three-and-a-half weeks ago.

What I mean is: Why didn't you call your family after you were robbed? Or after Tapachula? And hire a guide and go more comfortably. On the air-conditioned buses, she says.

It's complicated.

He looks out at the brightening day and the brightening land and with the yellow orb rising his spirits rise a little also. She is looking at him keenly, her face has opened up in this moment of new day.

My mother wanted me to wait with my great-aunt in Todos Santos.

Wait for what?

Until my lawyer could figure something out. Or until there is a reform of immigration law in the U.S.

Why didn't you?

I couldn't.

You couldn't wait?

I would have missed another semester at the university if I stayed much longer. And the laws might not ever change for someone in my situation. As things now stand, I can't legally return to my home or my family for ten years. I don't want to spend my whole fucking life waiting in a remote mountain village where the electricity cuts out several times a day, without the internet, or hot water, and living with my sixty-four-year-old great-aunt with whom I can hardly communicate because she only speaks our native language.

He falls silent. The day continues to brighten all around them. She doesn't press him, just looks out intently at the passing bushes and trees.

How could I? he says.

Your mother didn't understand?

My mother prays we'll find a solution through legal channels. She says I must be patient, have faith, a solution will present itself. But she's already spent half of her savings on my attorney exploring options that don't exist. I can't wait any longer. I'm already behind.

He sees a white truck driving alongside the tracks on a dirt road and a farmer with his cows in a field.

I miss them every day, she says.

He looks down at her profile. She too is looking at the farmer and he sees the sadness like an engraving in the new brackets around her mouth.

You can study at university even though you don't have papers? she says a few minutes later, surprising him with the question.

I received a scholarship for students in my particular situation. They call us "dreamers."

He falls silent for a moment.

I'm in my second year, he continues, right now my plan is to study economics or business, and minor in history, so I can get a good job when I graduate.

He laughs.

I live with my mom and my youngest sister who's still in high school. My older sister is a nurse, she moved out last year after she got married to an intern. And I had my girlfriend. It was a good life.

You have a girlfriend in California? she says.

We met last fall in an introduction to economics course.

Is she pretty?

Yes, he says.

He stares off into the fields again, looks at the sky, at the ever higher orb of the sun, and thinks how he doesn't want to talk about being a student at UC Berkeley or his family or about Antonia. I ought to only think *here*; think *northward*. But a new thought rises inside his mind: *perhaps it never existed*. Perhaps I dreamed that life and my classes and the orderliness of it, the ordinariness of the Bay Area and my routines, my studies and friends and family, because they are gone, immaterial now. Perhaps my life before the car accident on Interstate 80 when the cops took me into custody after I couldn't produce a valid ID and called Immigration and Customs Enforcement who came and put me in jail for months until I was deported and I arrived to Aunt Lourdes's concrete abode in the mountains with my green backpack and I felt so lonely and out of place; before I saw Antonia for the last time the morning of the accident in February because I wouldn't let her visit me in the detention center jail and so we haven't seen each other in months and have spoken only a few times on the telephone; before I was humiliated; before she phoned the last time and told me she had mailed a package with two paperback novels, a journal, a small keepsake, a photograph, and asked me why won't you let me visit you, Emilio? why don't you want to talk to me anymore?; before I was ashamed; before I felt so powerless and in despair—wasn't real. Perhaps this is the only reality: the moving train, the metal noise of its wheels, the heat and dirt and hunger and thirst and this girl next to me who is trying for something better, whose fortitude, whose beauty, whose body exists before me, and I am being irrational, I know it, it makes no sense, but it is upon me, in me from the moment I saw her standing at the banks of the Suchiate in a red tee shirt. Matilde, he says, do you have someone now?

I haven't wanted to have relations with anyone since my husband died, she says.

And then her face closes up tightly, the brackets retighten her lips, and she closes her eyes. She is gone for a time and Emilio feels sick and sad as the daylight continues to lift around them. The wind shifts and he can smell himself and Matilde and their stink. She looks younger in the yellow light and more vulnerable and he wonders: Is she the same girl from the Suchiate, am I the same man? They are both quiet and the older woman to his left continues sleeping, the train moves steadily. Matilde leans in against him and he feels his heart begin to beat a little faster in his chest. He is exhausted and anxious and hungry and uncomfortable and he is still, this force pushing against his reason, electrified when she is near: a current runs through him where she touches him. And to look at her—burnt skin and too thin and marked with insect bites and dirt, and to smell her body's secretions—is an unexpected comfort. He closes his eyes. He attempts to conjure Antonia in his mind. Sees her. She is unmarked by the sun, the insects, fatigue, by these difficulties in Mexico and in Central America, by financial hardship, by tragedy. He remembers her body, lithe and strong, how she often made him laugh when they were together. He puts his left hand into his pocket where the white stone lies small and cold and he holds on to it. He opens his eyes and with his right hand he reaches toward Matilde and takes the fingers of the hand she has just begun to pull on her hair with. He thinks for a moment that she too must feel it. He sees the broken nail on her index finger, the long lines of her finger bones, and the bright look of her when she opens her eyes and gazes at him now with her large dark eyes, the dark pools of her pupils, and the dark days ahead of them that remain a question, the continuously rising sun a beacon.

The train pulls into another town and comes to a full stop. Emilio and Matilde jump down and wait for the other three by the tracks.

I hope we can find a place to sleep here, she says.

We are in Ixtepec, Pedro announces once Jonatan and William have descended. There's a shelter a half mile from here where we can rest for a day. Eat a hot meal or two.

And bathe! she says. She smiles and she looks happier than Emilio has seen her look since Tapachula.

Royo jumps down and Emilio asks him if he is also going to the shelter for the night.

No, kid, he says, I'll wait here and take the next one out. I need to get back, my family is waiting for me. Maybe I'll see you across the line!

They shake hands and bid each other may it go well with you.

The five walk alongside the tracks, and as they leave the depot two police emerge and stop them before they can turn and run.

How much, Pedro asks.

Two hundred apiece, asshole, the policeman says, so that you know that in Mexico the train is not free. The other cop menacingly lifts the rifle slung across his chest by a few inches.

Pedro pays the bribe and the police say they can go. We are lucky they didn't take more, Pedro whispers when the cops are out of hearing range.

In twenty minutes they arrive at the front gates of the shelter and join the long queue of migrants waiting patiently outside. Each traveler is searched to make sure he doesn't carry weapons or drugs or alcohol. Emilio empties his pockets for the volunteer and shows him that he only has a small white stone in his pocket.

Once they are allowed inside the building, they are offered a meal of beans and rice and pork sausage in the large dining hall where an enormous statue of the crucifixion stands at the front of the room next to a smaller colorful painting of the Virgin of Guadalupe. Emilio sits with his friends and several other recently arrived migrants at a long plastic table and as he eats he thinks how simple fare has never tasted so delicious. Greasy, a little spicy, salty. It fills up his belly, sloshes around the empty sack with the cold punch that was also offered.

Grape punch has become my new favorite drink, he says.

His friends laugh.

Now who is the funny one of our little group? Jonatan says.

A cold beer would hit the spot for me, muchachos, Pedro joins in.

Matilde goes off to the women's area to bathe and the men shower and shave and brush their teeth. The shelter volunteers provide them clean clothes during their stay and the four men now stand in front of large concrete basins washing their traveling attire. When Emilio first submerged his shirt, underwear, and jeans into the cold water, it had turned black. He hangs his clean clothes to dry on the line and sees Matilde at another basin chatting with a few other women while she does her washing. She is wearing a close-fitting sleeveless top and he tries not to stare; her long hair hangs down her back, wet and shiny, and she appears more relaxed and at ease.

Dinner is called and they return to the now-crammed hall where upward of eighty travelers sit at the long tables eating soup and chicken. The father arrives and eats with them and after the meal he gives a short service in front of the statue of the crucifixion and says, I recommend you stay here, brothers, or return to your homes, there are too many dangers ahead, there is news every day of kidnappings.

As the father talks some of the recent arrivals fall asleep in their chairs or with their heads on the table, and his speech doesn't, because it can't, dissuade anyone from his, from her, purpose. He blesses them and bids them goodnight, and the five follow a volunteer to the rooms designated for sleeping where they find several unoccupied adjacent foam mattresses laid out on the floor. Emilio thinks how he has never in his life been more contented to lie on a quiet, flat, and immobile surface, safe and clean and stable and supine, his bare feet unhindered by shoes, his belly full from a hot meal. He lies next to Jonatan and falls asleep immediately. Matilde sleeps on Jonatan's other side.

What do you mean you can't go to the conference?

It's complicated, he said.

You ought to go. It's an honor to be invited as an undergraduate student. I can lend you the money if you need it for the airfare. Maybe we could even go together and take our first vacation as a couple!

No.

Why?

It's not the money.

My parents took my sisters and me to British Columbia on holiday two summers ago. It's beautiful there.

You're not listening.

It's beautiful!

I don't want to talk about this anymore.

You're my boyfriend, what is it, what aren't you telling me?

I'll tell you later.

No, here at Muir Beach. You said you loved me only a moment ago.

It was getting colder and the wind was picking up. He could see the thick band of greywhite fog hanging out at sea as it slowly began to advance toward them.

Please, she said.

We'll be covered by it soon, he said.

Tell me.

I didn't know when I was growing up.

Know what?

My parents didn't explain the situation until I turned sixteen and I insisted on getting my driver's license like my older sister.

But you don't have your license, that's why I drive us everywhere.

We left Guatemala when I was a baby and my parents sometimes talked about how bad things were, how the army targeted the Mam, and that was why we had to flee.

I'm sorry.

When I insisted for months on getting my license they finally told me why I couldn't.

This doesn't make any sense.

My dad didn't have his papers, of course that doesn't matter any longer. I don't either.

I still don't understand.

My mom and Susana have permanent residence and will get their green cards soon, and Brenda was born here so she's a citizen, but my dad and I traveled separately when we came from Guatemala. I don't remember, but we were apprehended at the border and they threw us back into Tijuana. We made it a few days later on the second try, but before Immigration sent us back to Mexico they stamped his papers and my papers with "removal."

We'll fix it.

No one in removal can legalize his status under current immigration law.

Your family lives here legally and you're not allowed to because of a fucking stamp? That isn't right. We must be able to fix this.

The wind was lifting and pushing against the two lovers walking on the beach. She was collecting small stones and small shells and the winter shadows fell inside their deep footprints on the sand, dappling the ground with dark on light. A quarter moon rose faintly against the light-blue January sky near the cliffs; the gulls glided higher and looked as though they were resting on air with their wings spread. She took his hand and pressed something into it.

I try not to think about it too much and continue to work toward my goals.

You're a student at one of the top universities and you just got invited to an international conference for a paper you helped our econ professor with. There must be an exception of some kind. Let's get married! she said, smiling.

It wouldn't make any difference in my case. No one can help me, not even my wife.

I'll talk to my dad, I'm sure he knows a good immigration attorney, or maybe someone at his practice can help and we'll get married, okay?

The fog covered the scene and darkened it, and he couldn't see any longer. He heard her saying okay? in echo against the formlessness, and although he tried he couldn't respond. His face was frozen and his lips.

He is disoriented when he first opens his eyes. His head aches, his mouth is dry. Where am I? He sees walls made of concrete blocks and a large room filled with foam mattresses covering the floor, dozens of strangers sleeping on them in their street clothes. There is a long window at the far end of the room near the ceiling with a crisscross of metal bars through which he can see a patch of blue sky. A small icon of the Virgin hangs below it. He sits up. His head is pounding. He turns and sees Matilde sleeping peacefully next to Jonatan in the sleeveless shirt she wore yesterday evening. He remembers: Ixtepec.

They depart after breakfast. They are all still tired, but the salve on their faces, the doses of aspirin for their aches and other pains, and their full bellies of hot food have bolstered them. They each carry a black plastic bag with a sandwich and a bottle of water the volunteers gave them. Pedro says they need to get out of the south quickly, give it their best, forward-going.

The day is warm and bright and humid. When the five arrive at the depot, the tracks are already covered with pods of migrants: hundreds wait as they do to catch the next northbound train. They find a small spot on the dirt and sit and in only two hours they hear the familiar air horn and see a massive locomotive approaching. What luck, Pedro says, we could have been stranded here for days. Hurry! he says, this one's going fast and not stopping.

The five run alongside the moving train with their black bags with the multitude.

Come on, the migrants already on board yell to those who are attempting to grab the ladders. Come on!

Emilio is beginning to breathe hard as he runs and the train cars pass him, one after another. Matilde gets ahead of him, and he sees Jonatan, who is taller than most of the other travelers, pulling her by the hand.

Then chaos ensues.

The Beast begins to leave the depot. Emilio is running and breathing hard and dozens of people around him and in front of him are vying for the metal ladders, pushing at each other, yelling epithets, struggling to make it aboard. Emilio darts ahead of two young women and a third who is pulling a small child by the hand and he grabs for a ladder, then stumbles and falls. He thinks, that's it, I'm killed or maimed, but he only hits the rocks hard on his knees and stands again, he has dropped his black bag, he runs. He can no longer see his friends, strangers surround and push against him, and his ankle turned when he fell and it hurts now as he grabs onto one of the last ladders on the last car. The horn blasts again and migrants above him yell their support, come on come on, muchacho, you've got it, don't let go, you can make it! Emilio swings one and then his second foot onto the ladder's rung as he heaves himself onto the crowded end of the hopper. The train leaves dozens of migrants and Ixtepec behind.

He climbs to the roof of the crowded boxcar. He doesn't see Matilde or the others on top of this one and he asks several of the men if they've seen a young woman with black hair with blonde streaks in it, slim, very pretty, and they say no they haven't seen her. He walks the length of the car and asks a woman holding a baby in her arms if she's seen his friends, four Hondurans, he says, and she shakes her head and he jumps to the next boxcar.

Be careful, man, you'll get yourself killed, one guy yells at him from behind, but Emilio is starting to panic and he is not listening to the warnings the travelers are yelling. What if I've lost them?

The train begins to pick up speed outside the town limits. He walks across the roof of the second boxcar, stepping between and around the prone and seated bodies that cover it to capacity. Some of the bodies say, slow down, muchacho, what's your hurry? He steps on a man's hand and the man yells curses at his retreating back as the great metal Beast moves forward, swings laterally like a monster as it rushes along the tracks. He jumps to the next wagon and he still can't see them. He is looking into the many tired faces and the many fearful questioning eyes (Is he a delinquent? Does he work for the cartel?), and he doesn't stop, or care, about their tired longings and abundant fear. He jumps onto a tank car next, it rounds down steeply on each side. There are only five migrants in the middle of this car, they hold on to a small circular metal railing. He slowly makes his way forward, afraid to slip and fall and be left behind in this godforsaken land. He says, I'm looking for a young Honduran girl with black hair with blonde streaks in it, to the five men who are staring at him intently. They are not sure if he's lying, if he hides a machete or a knife or a gun, and an older man says, No sir, we haven't seen that girl. They look at him with this trepidation and anxiety, and as he moves past them he says, Thank you, I'm only looking for her. He comes to the end of the tank car and sees a faded red boxcar and the train lurches. He loses his footing for a moment and falls to his knees and grabs hold of a protruding metal seam. The Beast's horn begins to blow loudly and the smoke is rising, the land moving from them. His heart beats so strongly in his chest now he is certain it strains against his sternum, hits his chest bone again and again as if to bruise it. Then he stands erect and without thinking he leaps to the old red boxcar and lands safely.

He traverses seven more cars. He sees the terrified faces, the dark pupils weighing him and his movements, and he is saying, I am looking for a pretty young Honduran in a grey hooded sweatshirt, have you seen her? And the travelers, ball-capped and tired and bedraggled and afraid of everyone who is lurking and moving too quickly atop the train cars, say no, no, sorry, we haven't seen that girl.

On the last car before the engine he recognizes the faded yellow cap they gave Pedro at the last shelter and lanky William who slouches next to him. Pedro sees him and yells, You are here!

Emilio makes his way toward them and when he finally sits down he realizes he is breathing heavily and his heart is still pushing furiously against his chest. He thinks he can see where the material of his tee shirt flutters near his chest bone because of it. Pedro offers him some water and he begins to calm down.

You okay? Pedro says.

Where's Matilde? He asks.

I thought she was on another car with Jonatan.

I walked the length of the train, I didn't find them, Emilio says, and he begins to feel sick: she's not on the train, they don't know where she is, maybe she is with Jonatan? She has to be with him.

They'll be on the next one, Pedro says, we'll wait in the next town. It's okay, she's not alone. Are you crazy, running up the whole cargo train?

Emilio doesn't say anything and looks out at the changing landscape. The green is coming on strongly now in Oaxaca, and his ankle, he realizes, is throbbing. His heart begins to pound less strongly in his chest and he is relieved to have found Pedro and William, but he is sick that he doesn't know what happened to Matilde. He makes a promise to himself that he will not let her out of his sight again—but what if they don't find them? What if I never see her again? And what if—and he decides he cannot allow himself to think in this manner, that he will drive himself crazy if he continues. He tries to concentrate on the green land passing by them.

A boy sitting near Pedro stands up and says he needs some exercise today too, and begins to skip along the top of the boxcar.

Several migrants yell at him to sit down and say he must be crazier than the jumper who just came up from the back. But the boy doesn't heed them and leaps to the car behind them, runs to a third car, then jumps back again several times yelling out with each landing that he is having too much fun to quit.

Most of the riders on the train top lie back and doze. Emilio can't relax; he is nervous and tense and he sits looking out at the land and sky with fixed eyes. The trees are covered in dark-green leaves and several carry pods of orange-eyed birds.

The boy finally tires of his antics and comes and sits next to Emilio, dangling his legs over the side of the car. Why is everyone so sleepy this morning? the boy says. Hey, so, he turns to Emilio, do you like Salvadoran beer or do you drink the Mexican crap? When I make it across the line I plan to have a six-pack of Pilsner.

The verdant earth all around, the heat of the day increases as the sun pounds down on them.

You want to know why?

Why what? Emilio says, glad for a distraction, the *what ifs* a barrage.

Why I'm gonna make it the whole way this time.

Emilio looks at the layers of dirt covering the boy's face, arms, and hands, at how his legs move up and down nervously.

I didn't the first try because the cops got me right after the Suchiate, and the second time they nabbed me in Mexico City when I wasn't paying attention. But now I know what I'm doing and I'll get a Pilsner for everyone when I finally make it across. You want to know how I know? What did you say your name was, the boy asks.

Emilio.

Emilio, did you grow up with your mom?

Yes, he says.

Yeah? the boy says. Mine's there in USA. In Florida. She went up to work when I was a little kid. She put my two sisters with my grandmother and she left me with an aunt. She thought a boy would be too hard on my grandmother.

The boy laughs.

I can't remember her face anymore.

The boy laughs again and Emilio can see the sad dark thing behind the boy's bravado.

I hardly saw my sisters, the boy continues. You have siblings?

I have an older sister and one younger than me.

Mine are older and lived across town and my aunt tried to care for me, but she had four kids. Mom would send a little cash, but months would pass sometimes with no money, so my aunt eventually resented me and said she couldn't keep me anymore and that's when I moved in with my youngest uncle and his girlfriend, I was nine, but the girlfriend didn't like me too much as I got bigger, and, ya know (he laughs), stayed out with my friends. Javier, she would say to me, if you run around with the bad ones you too will become a bad one. When she got pregnant they told me I had to leave.

Emilio is staring at the wall of green shrubs and trees; the air pushes against him and the train moves quickly now. The young Salvadoran boy speaks rapidly, unremittingly, his thin legs move up and down inside the tent of his baggy blue jeans continuously; his arms gesticulate. *What if they don't catch the next train? What if it takes days for another train to arrive?* Where did you live after that? Emilio asks.

I went back with my aunt but this time she made me stay outside behind the house, in a little shack. She said she couldn't trust me and yeah, I didn't go to school too much anymore, it was boring and the teachers would hit us, mostly they were interested in the pretty girls anyway. Then my uncle got me a job working with him at an auto shop. I made a little money and I hung out with my boys at night and my aunt didn't like that either, she would tell me I was stupid, and by then my mother wouldn't call us for months. She always called my grandmom's, so I was never there anyhow. And I started, yeah, to feel the pressure from the neighborhood boys who asked me to join their clica. Maybe for a little while I was even thinking it could be a good idea. (He laughs again.) Ya know? So that I could make real money, because the auto shop shut down when the owner couldn't afford to pay the weekly rent to the local boys for protection and what else was I going to do? Plus, at least when you're one of theirs, they take care of you, defend you. Ya know?

What if she's not with Jonatan?

But when one of the kids I grew up with was taken out, I

changed my mind. They got him outside his house (the boy makes a gun with his index finger and thumb and points it at the side of his head) in front of his mom and younger sister and grandmom. Pap pap pap. I decided after I heard the news that it was time for me to leave, time to go look for her. Because I knew it in my bones: she wasn't coming back. Everyone says they'll return in a year or two at the most, that they're just going to make some dollars, pay the bills, but they never do. No one ever comes back from the North. Maybe it's because they haven't made enough yet?

The boy laughs again.

I made the decision (the boy snaps his fingers sharply) like that, the day Martín was assassinated in the street. He was my age, fourteen, and I thought: I should go to her. Stop waitin' around. I had already waited eleven years. You had your mom? Well, when you don't have the love of your mom it's not easy. I could live without everything: without school or new clothes or the things she sometimes sent us, but I needed to see her again. Plus, things were getting hot in the neighborhood, people were dropping all the time. You'd see bodies in the street, walk by them on the way to the corner store. I was finding it harder and harder to remain independent.

The boy grins widely.

(What if she falls from the ladder of a moving train? What if we don't find them at the next stop in the next town like Pedro says?) I'm sorry, Emilio says, about your friend.

Thanks, old man. The thing is, it's not like I don't know why she left us. But still, I don't think she should have sacrificed us to take care of us. Ya know?

(No, I don't know. No, I don't understand. What if I made a mistake in leaving? What if she is lost?) Yes, he says.

This past year my buddies and I started trying things out and my aunt thought I was useless and she threatened to kick me out again. We had little glass bottles and she said she could smell the paint thinner on me when I got home. But we'd climb into the hills behind the house and Martín and a few other boys and I would get high overlooking the city while the sun would turn all the buildings orange and red and the sky would become a force, man, like in the movies, and that felt so good.

(*The spinning earth, the fast moving train, the loud noises of it, these men, this teenager, and we are on it, we cannot get off.*)

She doesn't know I'm coming, Javier is saying. I didn't tell anyone I was leaving because they will get you on the way out. Pap! So with twenty dollars in my pocket, this old pack, and the clothes I've still got on, I left the house and started walking. Now I don't even have one penny.

Javier is smiling again and he looks young, dirty, tired, too skinny and filled with determination and his tight bravado, and afraid like everyone else.

(*What if I don't see here again? What if I can't get it all back? What if hope is illusion? What if faith?*)

I'll make it because I waited to see her for so many years already, the boy says. And if I can be with her again I think life will get better. I know it! The Beast will take me all the way! Let's have a beer when we get across the line, shit, old man, we should have as many as we can consume. What did you say your name was again?

Emilio.

Emilio, we'll have a dozen Pilsner in the USA just like two fat bosses! And you can show me the American girls. Will you tell me how to start with them? What they like. How they dance.

What their favorite kind of music is. They say the American girls are less passionate than the Latinas: Is it true? And they're white. I like the dark girls, but it's okay, I can try the white ones! You got a white one, Emilio?

No, he says, no, I don't have anything.

You're joking, right? Javier says, and he laughs again.

A man with a blue tee shirt tied around his head stands up and yells out *la migra!* The word makes its way down the length of the train and upon hearing it the migrants jump to their feet and rush to the ladders and begin to climb down and jump off. The train begins to noticeably slow down and the travelers scramble and push. The pandemonium of hundreds descending, jumping, and falling onto their knees and getting up and running into the fields to hide, scattering the way birds take flight, but land-bound, ensues. Emilio rushes down the ladder behind Pedro and William and a dozen other men and jumps onto the dirt, hitting his knees hard against the ground, and rolling into the bushes. He stands and begins to run. His ankle is hurting but he is running as fast as he can. His heart begins to pound strongly in his chest once more and he loses Pedro and William and the afternoon is hot and God is not with him because he is not a believer, I am alone, he thinks, fleeing.

He knows because he was forewarned by Pedro and other migrants to get off before the immigration control and back on three-quarters of a kilometer farther down the tracks once the train has passed the checkpoint, otherwise, Pedro said, you'll have to wait in the bush for another train, which could take hours or days. The migrants have dispersed into the landscape among the bushes, and from behind Emilio thinks he hears gunfire. He sees the boy ahead of him and catches up with him and they run together.

I made it past this one last time, Javier says. Follow me.

The two scramble through the bushes. The branches and leaves slap at their bodies and shouts are heard and when they hear the train's horn blow they run even faster. Emilio is not thinking of his sore ankle or the hot sun or the green bushes or of his leg muscles burning and his pounding heart, he is following the quick and lithe Javier until they eventually come out onto the tracks. In moments they see the train barreling toward them and dozens of men burst from the brush and dash toward it and begin to clamber up the metal ladder attached to the outside of the train cars like so many armies of ants following invisible pheromone trails to the tops of the old sun-faded boxcars and hoppers.

The men already aboard yell you can do it, hurry up, hold on, hold on, to the travelers who run alongside the tracks and reach for the ladders. A few slip and fall onto the rocks; many will be left behind. Emilio is behind Javier and Javier grabs the rung of a ladder and climbs up and Emilio is next and grabs it, terrified as always of what could happen should he let go or slip and get pulled underneath, but he holds on strongly and pulls his body up steadily.

They climb to the top of a faded green boxcar and find a place and sit. They are breathing hard, their hearts pound, Emilio's ankle is throbbing and the wind is pushing into his face as the train picks up speed. He can see Pedro's yellow cap and William on the car ahead of him. He waves at them until Pedro finally sees him and waves back and Emilio is happy. Javier says, You made it, old man! And they both laugh.

An afternoon rainstorm soon arrives and the deluge increases until Emilio's clothes are soaked through to his skin. He holds tightly to the cooling metal of the boxcar while the rain falls upon them and I am in and of the elements, he thinks: the wind, the rain, the light of Oaxaca, the insects that bite and sting, the trees, the orange-eyed blackbirds, the land, the whole earth, wet and green and gleaming, goes by us, is upon us.

The Beast pulls into a small town and comes to a full stop. Emilio gets off with the rest of the migrants and finds Pedro by the tracks.

We'll wait for them here, Pedro says.

William, silent as ever, follows Pedro to a spigot to fill their water bottles. Emilio refills his bottle also and they all drink deeply as they wait for their clothes to dry in the sunshine. They are hungry and Emilio's stomach is growling as usual, but he is becoming accustomed to its complaints and he takes more large sips of water to quiet it.

A half-dozen vendors walk up and down the tracks with large plastic bowls filled with chips and crackers and cookies for sale.

Pedro says it's better to save their money and eat at the next shelter. The three sit on several abandoned wooden ties near the tracks and wait. Emilio sees Javier standing by himself and calls him to join them.

A lady gave me these at my last stop, the boy says as he kneels down, handing each of them a thin stale cookie from an open packet of half-eaten Marías.

This tastes so good right now, Emilio says.

It's not as good as a Pilsner but it hits the spot, eh? the boy says.

What I wouldn't give right now for one of those, Pedro says while he chews.

Now it's time for a cigarette, Javier says. He stands up. I think I'll stay here for a day or two and see if I can't make a few pesos in someone's garden, or cleaning up debris, and buy me some tobacco.

Take care of yourself, Emilio says.

You too, old man.

And when you get to your mom's in Florida, you could try an American one, Emilio says.

Javier promises he'll keep an open mind and turns and heads toward the town. Emilio watches his thin retreating back, notices how his empty pack hangs loosely from his slouched shoulders. He knows he won't see the boy again, and he hopes he will one day have his wish.

They hear church bells ringing in the distance.

It must be Sunday, Pedro says.

The three remain near the tracks, dirty and hungry and hopeful that a second train will arrive soon with their friends. They nap in the sun and their clothes by now have almost dried.

Emilio thinks about Matilde. He can't stop it. He is thinking and waiting and pushing down the what-ifs as soon as they rise to the surface of his thoughts. He closes his eyes and he sees her in his mind: the full lips and bright dark beautiful eyes, the straight nose and lovely smile, the light of her he can't explain that calls him to her. He imagines the girl he has known for only eleven days, detail by detail, in his mind, a distraction from *what if*. He puts his hand into his pocket, rubs the flat white stone with the pad of his thumb again and again.

He hears someone approaching and opens his eyes and sits up quickly. He sees an older, heavyset lady carrying two plastic bags and walking toward them. He knows he looks terrible: greasy hair and the insect bites on his face and dirty clothes and desperate soot-blackened hands and arms and neck. I look like any poor mendicant, he thinks.

This is for your journey, my son, the señora says as she hands him a plastic bag.

He opens it and sees a half-dozen sandwiches inside.

May God bless you, Señora, he says.

And you, she replies, and she walks away with the other bag of food for another group of travelers hanging from her hand.

The three savor the spicy bean filling on the soft white bread. They save the other sandwiches for later, for their friends, and continue the wait for the train. Emilio is still hungry, but not famished at least, and he lies down and dozes in the late afternoon sun, happy it's not raining, sweating, and thinking on top of his worrying of Matilde and of her *here*.

He saw the large dog sitting on its haunches at the river's edge. It weighed perhaps ninety pounds and its fur was grey and shiny like the bright stainless steel of dinner knives. The dog looked off into the distance to the other side of the brown river, toward the mountains which rose tall and menacing.

He approached the animal and sat down next to it. He was terrified, but he knew he must sit here and wait. He looked toward the other side of the brown river toward the mountains and he felt as if the insides of his body were held on a wire and attached to a winch and someone had turned the lever to pull his viscera tighter, but he wasn't certain who controlled the mechanism.

He looked down and saw that the invisible wire had now become two steel chains: one bound his ankles together and the other his wrists, as if he were a prisoner of war.

The dog turned toward him and on the left side of its head he saw a large, beautiful blue eye, and on its right instead of one, there were two smaller adjacent eyes, one dark brown, one green, and all three looked at him inquisitively. The dog now became less terrifying, for he understood the animal was blind. I was stupid to fear the large ineffectual monster, he thought.

The wail of a train horn startles Emilio, and when he opens his eyes he sees Pedro is already on his feet peering down the tracks. The sun is near the horizon, it must be almost six o'clock in the evening, Emilio thinks. The train slowly pulls in, full stops, and dozens of men and one older, grey-haired woman climb down and shuttle toward the water spigot. The riders appear tired and anxious and Pedro asks the grey-haired woman if something has happened and learns they were waylaid by an armed group in the countryside. They took our money and kidnapped a dozen migrants, including several young girls, the older woman tells him. Is there a shelter for us nearby? she asks.

Emilio panics and Pedro looks worried now. William wears his usual mask of disquiet.

The three walk the length of the train and continue to search among the new arrivals. The tops of the boxcars have all emptied and the new migrants sit alongside the tracks and on the abandoned wooden ties. They look dirty, apprehensive, hungry. There is no church-run shelter, no one to whom they can turn for protection, so they sit in groups of four and five or more and wait; those who managed to hide a little money purchase some food. Emilio feels his dread and worry augment.

What if they have her now?

They'll be on the next one, Pedro says optimistically, they could be on it.

The now familiar tightening in Emilio's body increases so

that he renotices what has not abated since he left Todos Santos, and even before that—since he boarded the airplane in Oakland for Guatemala, since he was first taken into police custody—the metal tool pulls the lining of his stomach and reaches for his throat, grabs his tongue, and he can't speak, he is vicious, tight, and scared (*what is happening where will this end where am I where is*)

William's voice interrupts his thoughts.

Look, over there!

Emilio turns and sees Jonatan pulling Matilde by the hand behind him. He sees the long red gash on Jonatan's face, healing but still ugly with the stark black stitches; he sees her gait and stature and slim form and dark hair with the blonde strands dyed into it and how she twists it with her free hand. She is looking down and she doesn't yet see them. She looks like herself, he thinks, her eyes and her mouth changed since Tapachula, the two new lines frame her lips, but she looks all right. She looks beautiful. Her face is sunburnt and there are several large mosquito bites on her cheeks, red and raised, and she is, as always, a vision. Then her black eyes rise and her gaze lands on his and an electric pulse passes from him to her or her to him, we are together again, he thinks, and a fluttering inside him loosens his tongue.

You are here! he yells.

She smiles and Emilio realizes in that moment then he has seen it only a few times since he met her. Once in the shelter in Tecún Umán after he was robbed and he complained about losing his Nikes, then after they boarded that first train in Bombilla, and when she learned she'd have a bath in Ixtepec, and now, and my God what is happening to me? How this attachment to the smile on this girl?

Uy, muchachos, Pedro says, we were worried, and he hugs Matilde.

We thought we lost you, Emilio says.

Jonatan describes how they couldn't grab that first train and this one stopped for thirty minutes, just long enough for him to see that one of the boxcars was open. I got Matilde and me inside it before anyone noticed and closed the door most of the way and jammed in a small piece of wood to keep the door from closing on us, he says. We slept until the train was detained and we were lucky, thank God, that the delinquents didn't look inside any of the cars.

The five sit reunited near the tracks and drink the water from their refilled bottles. Matilde and Jonatan eat a bean sandwich.

The sun has set and the three-quarter moon already rose into the dark blue sky. Night descends and the few electric lights of the depot come on.

We need to keep moving, Pedro says, it's gotten more dangerous everywhere.

They catch the same train when it leaves three hours later, although they cannot ride inside: a conductor checked all the boxcars and secured the doors before departing.

Emilio, Matilde, and Jonatan sit at the end of a hopper and the night is on them, the wind and the cold. They hug their sweaters and sweatshirts close to their bodies. Emilio has hardly spoken to Matilde since their initial exchange. He knows in a way it is better to speak less to her because he cannot stop thinking about her and he's not sure he can dissemble anymore. And sometimes he doubts that she can feel this electric pull and thinks maybe it's only in my imagination and my body and I can't dissemble so I don't think I should talk too much. He is trying to think about the months he spent with Antonia after they first met and fell in love and became boyfriend and girlfriend, but inevitably he starts thinking again of this girl's dark eyes, dark irises, the loveliness she invokes. Matilde sits next to Jonatan and leans into him and Emilio wonders if something has developed between them since Ixtepec. And in the places her body touches Jonatan's—her thigh and hip—he feels an imminent excitement in his own body, followed quickly by an unexpected feeling of rage. He knows he should try to sleep, he knows he is being stupid. He puts his head onto his bent knees. They are all shivering, and the night and trees and towns pass by them. The now small, bright-white moon has lifted high into the sky and it burdens him further as it marks the passage of the days on this long journey.

His rage increases.

He hates Jonatan. He hates her.

He knows he is building things up in his head, that the hard black beetle of his jealousy is crawling all over his thoughts. *I could throw myself off this train. I could return to Todos Santos. I could do something crazy.* He tries again to sleep. He tries to unbuild what his mind is making. He wonders if his mother and sisters are looking up at the moon tonight at home, if they wonder how he is, where he is. He stares at the white dot hanging high above him and he thinks how space is treacherous and betrays us and how all of us on this earth, despite what we think and whom we love and inside which countries we hold official papers of nationality, lie vulnerable beneath the moon's bright unsettling light and forces.

Black and black until the darkness on the eastern edge of the sky imperceptibly blues and then slowly begins to white-yellow. The vast bowl of the sky lightens and the forms take form on the land again, or perhaps the land itself slowly emits the light: the inverse of the shuttering of the previous night and Emilio can see clearly once more. Another dawn. He is becoming familiar with the intervals of sundown and sunrise when the contours of the earth are less sharply delineated, color is more richly hued, and despite his discomfort and the constant trepidation, he finds the light's diminishment, its increase now with each moment, to be nothing less than wondrous.

The land rushes by them, through mist and smoke, high clouds crisscross the sky. Fields of corn and sugarcane and banana plants emerge. A small town with red tile roofs and white buildings appears in the distance and they are in the state of Veracruz.

If I still had my things, my journal and ballpoint pen, he thinks, I could record the passage of the days. He thinks about the old green backpack he used for years in high school and in college that was with him when he was arrested, of his blue jeans and baseball hat, and of the novel Antonia sent him because she thought it might entertain him during his wait in jail. Who wears my clothes, my red cap; who can read *Great Expectations* in English? Did that fat cop keep the wristwatch my mom gave me? Does the pedicab driver wear my Nikes or did he sell them because they were the wrong size? He regrets again what he has lost.

Jonatan gets up and goes to the end of the car where the migrants give each other privacy to urinate. Afterward he says he's going to ride up top with Pedro and William. I'll continue to work on my suntan, he jokes. You two stay down below.

They watch the palm trees and lush fields in the countryside move by them. Emilio's stomach is growling again. When I get home, he thinks, I will eat as many plates of chicken, black beans, and tortillas as my mother will serve and the next day we'll go out for Italian, that's what I feel like eating this morning, and I'll order two portions of spaghetti and meat sauce and garlic bread and a big piece of chocolate cake to finish the meal and cold water in every glass every day and the best sourdough baguettes from Acme Bakery with sweet butter for a snack later.

The last time I made it this far the only friendly ones were in La Patrona, a Salvadoran sitting near them says. The ladies who prepare food. We should pass through the town some time this morning.

They cook for us? Emilio asks.

You'll see, muchacho, a hot meal can't be too far ahead.

Not more than an hour later they approach another town and the train begins to slow. The horn blares.

Attention! yelled out from above.

Attention! yelled several more times.

Get ready, the Salvadoran says to them.

Everyone stands up at the ends of the hoppers and on all the surface areas of the cargo train.

Emilio and Matilde lean their torsos over the railing and see dozens of old ladies and young women and small children with their arms stretched out toward the incoming locomotive. Each of the hands holds a black plastic bag or two water bottles tied together at the neck. Emilio leans out as far as he can without falling and extends his arm, opens his hand. There is a festive air upon the travelers, it rises in everyone, buoyant and expectant.

Las Patronas! they say, the ladies who give food, water, and love to the migrants on the cargo trains.

Emilio catches hold of a bag from an older señora and yells out his thank you, drops it onto the metal floor next to him, and thrusts his arm out once more. The train continues moving steadily and blows its horn a third time and when he turns his head to look behind him he sees that the older señora already has another bag of food offered for the next traveler. He looks for something more but misses the bag a young woman extended toward him; he catches two bottles of water strung together from a young girl instead. He tries for one more bag and misses it. Matilde, he notices, has gotten one. As they near the limits of the town he sees a young boy sprinting alongside the tracks near them, clutching something in one of his hands. Emilio stretches his arm toward the boy but the boy can't quite reach him and runs faster, Emilio extends his torso and arm out even farther, and when their fingers finally touch the gift is exchanged, from an unknown child to an anonymous migrant, Emilio thinks.

Enjoy it! the boy yells as the train pulls away from him.

I will, Emilio says, smiling, and he notices the movement on his face and realizes how he also has not smiled very much these past weeks, and how charity in reality is very simple: a piece of fruit from a boy's hand; a black plastic bag filled with baggies of warm rice and beans from a señora's. Water.

Let God carry you North, another grey-haired señora in a wheelchair yells by the side of the tracks as the Beast leaves La Patrona. She hands bags of rolls piled on her lap to three young children who hurl them up to the men on the roofs of the wagons one after the other.

Emilio looks up and sees that Jonatan, who stands next to William, has by some miracle caught two bags of food and four water bottles tied together at the neck, which he now holds aloft his head.

¡Viva Mexico! he shouts joyously to the sky.

Everyone laughs. All the Central Americans who ride the Beast northward through this foreign and dangerous country. Even the normally taciturn William looks at ease and smiles for a moment as the train pushes into the countryside once more.

Matilde and Emilio climb to the top of the hopper and join the others to share their repast. The rice is salty and delicious, the tortillas soft and warm, the refried beans are spiced with chiles, and the cooked food makes them all contented. The atmosphere on the train remains optimistic for a time.

The Mexicans are in a good mood this morning, Jonatan jokes.

How much farther is it? Matilde asks.

We cross Veracruz first and then climb the mountains to Mexico City. Four more days at the most, Pedro says. You feel okay?

She is silent. She eats the tortilla and when Pedro asks her another question she replies in monosyllables after that.

The train advances, its loud metal wheels screech and clank and the horn blows three times when it enters another town.

I'm going down below again, she says.

I'll go with you, Emilio says.

There is no question now of him leaving her side. She doesn't say anything and Pedro, Jonatan, and William don't comment. The two descend. There are only a few women on this train, and the men will always make room for her at the end of a hopper. He doesn't say much to her and she is generally quiet, as if she uses most of her energy to keep going, to hold herself together, as if words were a currency she must carefully allocate.

She sees green banana leaves, tall palms, grey clouds that hang on the mountains, but the worry is so strong in her that often it is the only sensation she perceives. She is thinking about the two she has left behind. What is Katerin doing? And Jorge Luis? She misses her children's bodies and she has never, since their births, been so far from them. She trusts Pedro will get her across the line and she will find work and she will be able to care for them and they will be secure. She only has to give it her best. She is tired and sore and uncomfortable, but at least we have had some food, she thinks. The day is passing; the green land. She can see the massive waxing moon begin to lift from the horizon. Emilio asks her if she sees it and she turns to look at him. His dark skin is a darker brown now and burnt from the sun; his thick black hair stands on end; his full lips are dry and chapped; his black eyes are red with fatigue. He has his hand in his pocket as he usually does fingering the stone he carries. He seldom looks at her and he doesn't talk very much in his sometimes Mexican, sometimes American, accent, but she can feel him when he is near. When you gaze at me intently I can sense it, other times, a small animal stares from the wild corners of your tired black eyes into the distance, she thinks.

Emilio.

Yes, he says, and turns toward her, surprised to hear her voice after a long interval.

Thank you.

147

For what?

For Tapachula. She turns her head and looks out again at the countryside and the train is loud and constant and shrieks around them. They both sit quietly throughout the late afternoon.

The sun begins its descent and the migrants on the top of the train are relieved of the sun's rays on their heads and arms and backs. The wide fields extend out from the Beast's body, a flat inert extension of the Beast's rage and speed. Night approaches.

Emilio hears someone yelling from above and, like all the riders, he feels a steep rise in his trepidation: that the police are ahead in the distance, or narcos or the migra, or a gangster is aboard the train.

Look up!

He stands and leans out of the car and sees a man on the adjacent boxcar pointing to the sky above them. The sun is setting, deep red fills the horizon, the moon has risen, and European starlings in a flock of a thousand birds lift as one from a cornfield as the Beast roars by them. Come see, he tells her, and she joins him at the metal railing.

The flock breaks into three groups that now move in circles, crisscrossing one another. The iridescent black of the bird bodies, the blue of the sky, the red and yellow of the crepuscule, and the yellow moon converge as the birds swing around, push into and out of one another, turn the evening into a wild circumlocution of black on red and blue and yellow. It is like watching the vigorous vertiginous movement of waves on a canvas of the air, Emilio thinks.

Now a black wall of birds rises, now it crashes into the adjacent flock, now the two become one column of upward black-bodied speed, fall to the earth but do not crash into it, swing across the land like a sheet of water skimming the side of a wall, then lift again moving upward as one: a tower ascending and descending. During the ruckus there is never a collision, the murmuration flails the air and makes it, or it makes them, one large united animal being.

As if God Himself were among us, the Salvadoran now standing next to Emilio says.

He will be with thee, he will not fail thee, his young female companion says.

How do they do it? Matilde asks.

It's their nature from thousands to become one, this is their only defense against the larger hawks and falcons that prey on them, the Salvadoran says.

They make such pretty pictures in the sky! Matilde says.

That one looks like a fish, Emilio says.

Or a dog's elongated snout!

Now see, they've become a black plume rising, the young woman says.

The train moves forward and the flock of starlings is left behind, it will be cold soon in the darkness.

I am unable to write anything down, Emilio thinks during the long course of the night when he can't sleep, but I can see, I can listen. To this night. To the wind. To the Beast who talks nonstop in her diesel tongue, her susurrations, her throaty clanks and squeaks and mournful horn blowings. To the migrants and their stories, their strange accents and lexicon, to the looks on their tired and burned faces before darkness descends in its full armor. To the blue in the sky. To the falcon who would rake its talons down my spine. To the fields of sugarcane and maize and the Mexican villagers walking alongside the train tracks, bathing in the mountain streams and in the lowland swimming holes. To the federales whom no one can trust, the municipales and the migra, young gangsters and the narcos. To the canopy of stars above, bright-hued and infinite in their number, seemingly untroubled by the small planet they surround. To the bright dangerous beauty of every moonrise. To my stomach and its constant complaints and its eventual quiescence. To the bites on my face; the blisters on my feet; sore ankle, sore ribs; my hands, cold, dark, and burned; the once-lighter band of skin beneath my old wristwatch. To Guatemala to Honduras to Mexico and El Salvador. To Javier and Royo. To the golden light at dusk and each subsequent spectacular pink dawn. To the starlings in their black sky dance. To this dark-haired girl sleeping at my side with the dark iris and dark pupils and the new brackets that gently frame her beautiful full mouth. He looks up at the star-filled vault and it presses down on him. To the starlight. He looks back at the girl. The invisible light within.

And he thinks he could even listen to God.

I listen for Him in the open field of night.

Silence.

He was on the bus on the brown road on the brown cliffs, the brown abyss stretched out below him. The road curved ahead sharply and the cliffs descended steeply. He was driving the Blue Bird and its exterior shone bright blue and green against the dun-colored earth. The bus leaned into the void and he pulled tightly on the steering wheel to right it and continued driving forward. He knew he should not tarry here, he must only advance. He was afraid because he didn't know how to drive the large bus, but he didn't speak of his fear to the passengers. Someone in back yelled at him to turn on the radio. Central Americans wearing baseball caps and carrying black backpacks and black plastic bags filled the seats. They had come from all over the region with their black eyes, black and brown and blond hair, sun-darkened and burnt skin; their diverse idioms.

Turn on the lights, Matilde said, we can't see.

Where are you? he said.

The road twisted again sharply and the bus tipped at an angle and he pulled strongly on the steering wheel and hoped they would make it to the straightaway without delay and to the aqueduct awaiting them with its clear, clean water.

Where did you go? he asked.

Put the radio on damn it, someone yelled from the back, and he thought it might be his mother because the voice was speaking in Mam, although his mother never used profane language that he could recall.

Where did you go? he repeated.

I want to hear that norteña music. I want to drink a beer and relax.

Was that his father's voice? Was it Pedro's?

The orb of the sun makes its appearance in the east and a small joy rises in him again for the yellow star and the rebirth of day. The train is crossing more green fields and more mountains hold the distant sky, more small towns dot the landscape.

I have not spoken with anyone in my family in almost two weeks. They don't know where I am and I often, also, don't know. In the middle of the state of Veracruz, at least a thousand miles from the border with the United States, and several hundred more from there to Berkeley, he thinks.

Emilio observes Matilde in the new light of morning as she sleeps next to him. She has the hood of her sweatshirt pulled tightly around her face; her arms and legs are tucked into her body. He looks at her and thinks about the mask he wears on his own face with its tightened corners near the eyes, the furrow in the brow, the indirect pupil gaze in a futile effort to protect itself from outside forces; the compressed lips. He knows, in fact, that he wears a mask not because of any mirror but because he sees it on her and on the other migrants. The dawn returns her to me and she is getting thinner every day, becoming smaller, pulling into herself, becoming a reason coupled to the one I began with. She opens her eyes now and looks at him darkly.

Matilde, he says, his voice coming out from the long tunnel of silence during the hours of the night.

Yes?

We can talk.

She puts her face closer to his to hear him more clearly above the din of the train, the metal wheels, the clattering and clanking. Two women sleep soundly to her left.

He pulls her hood away from her ear and he puts his mouth near it and smells her hair and its oils and behind her neck, the sweat and dirt. He smells the days upon them, the countryside, the smoke, the weather, the moving air.

I can't help it, he says.

What is it? Everything okay?

I can't stop it.

Stop what?

I am falling in love, he says against the skin of her neck, first in English, and then in Spanish.

She pulls away from him. She pulls the hood back over her ear. She turns and gazes at the landscape and the loud machine rocks them and fills them with its commotion. She doesn't say anything and he is feeling chagrined now, he stares off into the green fields and wishes he could retract his words for he knows they were stupid, intrepid, made by the long days and nights of traveling and by the night in Chiapas when he carried her with her blood on him, her weight against him, and he became in this way, although he didn't understand it immediately, obliged. He is bound to her. His hand is in his pocket and the small white stone lies there with its tactile, mineral comfort, and he rubs his thumb across it.

She begins to speak to him after an interlude. She has pulled the hood back from her face and she looks at him. She speaks close to his ear.

I can't tell my family, I can never tell them, she says. There were three. One held the gun to my head so that I would not move and I was very afraid and I would not have moved so he didn't need to keep his gun pressed to the side of my head but he kept it on me the while. They used me like an animal. They bit my back, my shoulders, and the man pressed the gun against my temple or into my cheek. Each night as we travel I am relieved to know my children are home with their grandmother, in a bed, sleeping soundly, and safe. But their mother is not me any longer.

The words fall into his ear canal and slide into his stomach and Emilio feels sick and saddened.

I understand it wasn't my fault, she says, that they were criminals. I knew of the risks to girls before we started the journey and I took the necessary precaution for this month of travel.

She presses her lips together tightly, folds one against the other, and thins them in this manner.

But they made me bleed that night like a virgin beneath the ceiba tree.

She pauses.

The tree was almost bare of leaves, its branches covered in the undergarments of the women they had taken there before me. The man with the gun boasted of the numbers of girls he had raped in that location already. Bras and underpants of every color and size like souvenirs.

She rolls her lips together again and like this she is able to speak a phrase and then another without crying.

(I pissed myself in the dirt, Emilio thinks, not a child of God, but an animal held down by his terrors.)

They hung mine there proudly after they finished. Do you understand what I'm saying?

He looks at her closely.

An old Matilde was left beneath the ceiba tree with her underclothes, with her old life, her old joys. A muchacha she used to be.

I can't help it, he says.

She leans back against the metal wall of the hopper and closes her eyes. She appears to be dozing again and he notices where the unrepressed tears wetted her cheeks and her chin despite her efforts.

I've fallen in love with you, Matilde. I find you beautiful in every way.

She remains quiet and where her body presses against his thigh and arm, he feels its natural pulse.

The rain comes down in white sheets. The sky is grey-white and the temperature has dropped. He lies atop the boxcar underneath a small plastic poncho with Jonatan and a Honduran called Rigoberto. He is drenched and shivering. Pedro has come down with a cold and Emilio agreed to leave Matilde's side so Pedro could have shelter from the storm, but he is worried now because he promised himself he wouldn't leave her and he has left her for Pedro's sake and although he wants to keep his word it is already difficult. Jonatan is recounting an anecdote of when he and his brother were children and they ate wild mushrooms in a wood: I didn't realize the mushrooms were hallucinogenic until my brother began yelling son of a bitch at the sky, at the air, because he thought it was falling down on us, Jonatan laughs, and the world was ending.

The metal train moves along the metal tracks in the unremitting weather. The flimsy plastic does little to shield the three men and Emilio wishes he were riding inside the boxcar, or that there were space for him down below on the hopper, and he thinks how until now he has always loved rainfall, grey fog, cold summers, but from behind glass, inside warm buildings, in a car with the heat turned on high. Now I hate its relentless barrage, its reminder that we are nothing, exposed and beaten by the storm waters on our skin-vulnerable bodies.

Watch out for the electric wires, a voice yells out.

As the message makes its way down the locomotive the travelers tuck their heads, man to man to woman to avoid them. The train whistle is blowing, the wheels crank, the passengers lie prone and shivering and clutch the metal grates. Jonatan is telling every sordid joke he can think of to entertain and distract his companions and keep them awake and alert. Rigoberto laughs easily at his countryman's antics. They all know fatigue loosens their grip, closes their eyes, remains an enemy.

Another hour passes and the rain finally lessens and then abates altogether. Blue patches of sky return. The sunshine begins to slowly warm them and dry their clothing. The Honduran pulls out a few stale tortillas and Emilio shares his remaining baggie of rice and the fruit he had saved for last. William passes around a bottle of water, and the four are happy for the rice tacos, a piece of orange, and relief from the weather. The abundant green stalks of maize spread out from the tracks, and the leaves look a brighter shinier newgreen.

The day passes slowly. They enter and leave one town after another, the air horn blows. Pineapple bushes now surround them on all sides. Most of the men sit quietly or doze. Emilio is hungry again and he is bored. Rigoberto sits next to him and like him looks out at the land.

The north of Carolina, the Honduran says when Emilio asks where he's headed.

Emilio looks at the holes in the side and bottoms of the man's worn tennis shoes, at his tanned brown face where the travails of his life have left deep lines in his forehead and between the eyes, at his scarred calloused hands; in the front black quadrant of his mouth three teeth are missing.

What's taking you there? Emilio asks.

I'm joining a neighbor's son to paint houses.

Where did you come from?

It's called Lazos de Amistad in the department of Comayagua, Rigoberto says, and he speaks slowly and deliberately like all the Hondurans from the countryside Emilio has met, as if each phrase were a caution. Do you know our department?

No.

It was a good place for years until Mitch came.

Who was he?

Not a he but a what that arrived to the village at the dinner hour. I opened my front door and walked outside with my baby in one arm and the three-year-old was holding my other hand, my wife had the oldest two, and it took the house from behind our backs. It took everything. The chickens, two goats, and our mare from her stall. All of our possessions.

I'm sorry, Emilio says.

Today's small storm was nothing by comparison. After that, we lived in one room I built with my two oldest boys from concrete blocks and a tin plate the government gave us for the roof.

Rigoberto stops talking and Emilio waits for him to continue.

Why did you finally decide to leave?

I decided, Rigoberto continues in the slow melodic cadence of his region, to abandon Lazos de Amistad because in that place we now live like the animals.

The sun beats on their bodies, the wind takes some of the heat with it. Row upon row and mile upon mile of low-lying pineapple plants fill up the fields.

When God first made the earth it was new so everyone had to live like that, but this was many thousands of years ago. After Mitch my family lived that way again, and in that room my children learned the burden of a day's hunger.

You asked why, muchacho, Rigoberto says, and I'll tell you: it's because I finally concluded my family ought to have a day that hasn't worried the monies owed. If there will be food for dinner. They ought to have their basic necessities, and the little ones ought to attend school because the fees have been paid. We ought to purchase the medicines if one of them takes a fever.

(The old rain, the beating sun, Emilio thinks, the girl down below, this old farmer before me.)

In the world we live in now the rich man only wants to get richer. The rich doesn't care about the poor man, so there's no solution for us there.

Rigoberto stops speaking again. Emilio listens, waits for the voice to resume.

We never recovered after it came to the village, he says, so when my youngest took sick and my señora and me couldn't afford the medicines or to bring a doctor or take him to the clinic in town and he died in the bed in her arms then I knew

(Pain its own cadence.)

that I wasn't a man of the house any longer. That I had to abandon them in order to be a good husband, a good father. The neighbor's boy went up five years ago and he lives in the north of Carolina painting big houses and his job pays nine dollars an hour. My señora didn't want me to go, she said it wasn't good to leave her and the children and the children cried when I left them, but I'm sure we'll have something better again if I can make nine. In Lazos de Amistad you might not have that in a whole week.

Rigoberto falls silent. He eventually lies down next to William and sleeps.

Emilio stares out at the land and watches the afternoon wane. They ride past fields of bananas, more pineapple bushes, stalks of maize, and tall palm trees. The light moves brighter and hotter upon them, their clothes dried out and stiff in the sunshine and wind, their faces and arms burning. They pass through small towns and the air horn wails three times. When I worked at Acme Bakery I took my fill of baguettes and shortbread cookies home after each shift, Emilio thinks. I made twelve–fifty an hour. I am so hungry again, I want a glass of cold water for my thirst. I wish this day would quickly find its end.

The Beast begins to slow down in the middle of the country-side. There is no town anyone can see and the air horn doesn't blow. Hundreds of bodies atop the boxcars and hoppers tense up hoping that the train is only temporarily losing speed. The train finally comes to a standstill alongside a dirt road and a fallow stretch of field.

Without the noise of the locomotive, the earth comes to life in Emilio's ears. He hears the loud frogs in the field and from the invisible watershed. The birds singing their various trills and songs. There is a strange insect sound he has never heard before and it fills the air. The late afternoon concert opens around them punctuated at short intervals by the heaving sounds of the train's brakes. Emilio's anxiety increases as each minute passes. He stands up and sees Jonatan chatting enthusiastically one car ahead of them with a former combi driver he'd worked with in Tegucigalpa and who he'd gone to catch up with. Emilio waves his hand to attract his attention without success and then tells William he's going to go look for Matilde, but when he turns he sees her and Pedro already ascending the ladder. She says, What do you think it is?, and they sit down together. Pedro is still sick-looking and coughing. The train engine is quiescent and the brakes heave, the frogs and birds and insects make their melodic and strange noises, and the migrants wait, expectant and uncertain, a wire of trepidation holding all of them attentive.

Maybe it's a problem with the motor, Rigoberto says.

They hear the sounds of car engines. Within minutes a caravan of police cruisers, black four-wheel-drives, and a large white tractor trailer come into view on the dirt road. The vehicles pull up and stop next to the train. The windows of the four-wheel-drives are black-tinted and opaque.

Car doors open and a cop yells out, Don't move, sons of bitches. Policemen with ski masks covering their faces quickly spread out along the tracks on each side of the six-car train. The policemen point their assault rifles at the migrants on top of the boxcars and at the ends of the hoppers.

If you move, we'll get you.

A half-dozen men wearing military uniforms descend from the black vehicles, their faces also covered with black ski masks, and each carrying an AK-47 at his side. They wear tennis shoes on their feet in place of army-issued boots.

A low phrase runs atop the freight train now like a line of fire: *The Señores are boarding us.* The cartel no one even dares mention by name.

Emilio hears it as Matilde grabs him by the arm. She leans into his body. The migrants huddle together as best they can and hope by holding on to their groupings of five and ten atop the train cars that there will be some safety in their numbers.

Two of the uniformed masked men climb the ladder behind the engine, three cars ahead of them. They reach its top and point their weapons at the migrants, yelling Get down, motherfuckers. Stand up, move it, get the fuck off, now! The men and women on the first car rise together and move toward the ladder like a small animal herd. They descend quickly, the guns on them, their fear driving them. Piece of shit, what are you doing? one of the masks yells at a man who has bent down to adjust his shoe and holds up the line momentarily. The loud report of a gun ruptures the air. The mask orders two other migrants to throw the body off the boxcar and it hits the ground heavily. The remaining passengers disembark in a full panic.

Once the first car has emptied, the two masks jump to the second. Get up, motherfuckers, get the fuck up and move it motherfucking Central American bitches. When they shoot a second man in the stomach the loud gunshots drown out the animal noises of the countryside for a moment. The remaining migrants disembark as quickly as they can. Down below, soldiers load the migrants into the white tractor trailer with their guns and curses. One wide-eyed body is unmoving on the ground, and the second body bleeds and twitches on the metal grate of the second car.

Emilio can't see Jonatan amid the more than three dozen men and women; many hold their heads in their hands and pray loudly and ask for mercy. The two masked men jump to the third car swearing and shoving and pointing their assault rifles, saying move it pussies, dirty fucking Indians, get the fuck up or we'll kill you right here. The terror is on everyone and the migrants are moving quickly, a woman cries out, and then Emilio sees the back of Jonatan's head, he is taller than most of the others, he stumbles toward the metal ladder with the group. The frogs are croaking and the birds are stuttering; another woman screams loudly down below. Emilio pushes Matilde beneath his thighs. She is praying, talking below her breath: Mother of God, dear God, help us Lord, please protect us, Señor Jesus. He covers her with his body as best as he can, tries to hide her, and he has never prayed and God for him is no God and he is saying to himself: help us, somebody, who can do it? And he begins talking to his dead father: help me, Papá. Papá, please, if you can. And to his mother: I'm sorry I'm sorry I'm so sorry. Then he can't find Jonatan from where he sits, he can't see him any longer.

Terror makes him blind.

The three boxcars ahead are emptied of travelers except for the now lifeless body on the second car in the late afternoon in the state of Veracruz. Black and green plastic bags and abandoned backpacks and discarded items of clothing and other detritus lie scattered across the tops of the train. The women and men at the ends of the hoppers down below are being loaded into the white truck. The two masked men stand at the ready to jump onto the fourth car.

You're next, assholes, one says.

I will disappear into this blind country and I don't want it, Emilio thinks, I don't. All of it beyond my scope and power and I am only trying to get home. He hears Matilde's prayers and the rest of the men pleading their Gods and Señor Jesuses and Holy Virgencitas, Mother of God, protect us.

From below someone yells, It's filled.

Take out the rest of them, another says.

And then Emilio knows it: he's going to die today amid the unfamiliar insect sounds and the bright green land and in a country he did not know and knowing now only its bleakest underbelly. Matilde hides underneath his body and perhaps in lying on top of her she will not perish and I won't see my mother and my sisters or Antonia and home again and I am sorry, Mamá, he thinks, to cause you this pain. I was foolish. I didn't understand what I was getting myself into and stupid and arrogant and thinking only to have things as they were, as they had always been. He knows that he will be lost, he will disappear with the untold stories of this day, pass away and join the voiceless patrimony of the unrecorded dead. He hears Pedro saying goodbyes to his wife, Ana, and his children, and poor terrified

William at his side, huddled next to him and sobbing. Matilde's body shakes uncontrollably beneath his.

He hears the door of a vehicle loudly slam shut and a hush descends among the armed men. Emilio lifts his head slightly and sees a middle-aged man standing next to a black SUV; large reflective sunglasses cover his eyes. Unlike the others, he wears a bright yellow polo shirt pulled tightly over a fat belly and tucked into pressed blue jeans; cowboy boots. He is smoking a cigarette, and once he's finished it he tosses the butt on the ground near the dead migrant.

God damn it, he says, and he now fiddles with an object in his hand.

My fucking lighter is out of gas.

He throws the plastic lighter onto the ground and looks up at the train. Emilio ducks his head.

You imbeciles get the fuck down, he says. I told you earlier we leave as soon as we are at capacity, I've got other appointments on my calendar this afternoon.

The two armed men stand no more than ten feet from the migrants who desperately hold themselves to the metal grate of the fourth car. Emilio can see their dark eyes through the holes of their masks, he can hear their loud breathing. Matilde shakes so much beneath Emilio she moves his legs violently. One of the black masks says, We'll get you fucking niggers next round. The two men turn and descend the ladder.

Someone has closed and secured the two large doors of the tractor trailer. The boss has already climbed back into his car. The armed men get back into their black vehicles and the police into the patrol cars.

Oh God, oh God, Jonatan, Pedro says.

The white tractor trailer starts its loud diesel engine and turns around, and the SUVs with the black windows drive one in front of and two behind it. The police cars escort the caravan from the scene.

The Beast's engine starts up (the engineer no doubt received a bite for his assistance) and drowns out the frogs and unfamiliar insects and birds' songs once more. The train slowly begins to move forward and Matilde is crying hysterically and the men are all silent and doomed and terribly relieved to be leaving this place. A few of the men have pissed themselves, Emilio smelled its acrid scent around him before the train began to move and he is happy he did not soil himself today.

We are okay, Pedro finally says, as he coughs and wheezes. But oh God, Jonatan.

Matilde sits up and wipes her face and tries to compose herself. Where are they taking him? she asks.

A Guatemalan sitting behind them says he heard they keep them at a safe house until their relatives can wire the ransom money.

Do you know how much they ask for? Emilio says.

I've heard it's a few thousand dollars, the Guatemalan says. Sometimes the women work as girlfriends if they can't afford it.

What if a man can't pay? Rigoberto asks quietly.

Emilio puts his arm around Matilde openly and holds her tightly. The wind and the absent noises of the frogs, of the strange insects, the loud hammering of the steel wheels, the smoke in his eyes, and the mournful horn of the Beast are all inside of him severely. She holds him back in their embrace. The wind makes them shiver, reminds them they are still free.

Poor Jonatan, she whispers, I hope they will call his wife soon.

We have to get out of the south, Pedro says.

As the train begins to move at higher speeds, the bags and jackets and other items fly off the abandoned cars. The corpse of the unknown traveler falls into the countryside.

Night descends. The men and women riding the Beast are cold and quiet tonight. The full moon rises with the setting sun and Emilio can't help but wonder if the beautiful satellite somehow brought this ominous day upon them.

Watch out for the branches, brothers, a call travels down the train car. Emilio lies flat on his belly next to Matilde, the air and darkness and the branches above rush by and hit against them.

The air horn interrupts the night at intervals in its round of three as they enter small towns and depart them.

She has fallen asleep and her body is twitching. He is holding onto the metal grate and his legs are on top of hers to secure her as best he can. The clouds clear or the train moves out of a clouded into an unclouded landscape, and the incandescent sheet of stars spreads out less brightly because of the moon. There is the continuous loud clanking of the boxcars and metal wheels, the blare of the horn, and the men who cling to the back of the Beast as she moves them northward. He lets Matilde sleep for a time with his vigilance upon her, but when the train begins to lean sharply from side to side he says her name to awaken her. He doesn't want to take the risk, he worries he won't be able to catch her in time if she begins to slip away from him.

She emits a soft cry of distress when she finally opens her eyes.

You must wake up and hold on now, he says.

When the train's movements even out and there is a calm spell, she falls asleep again between his legs.

He saw the back of her head in the dimness, the dark hair lying against the shoulder blades, the scapulae like wings pushing against her skin and the fabric of her tee shirt: an etching of the invisible hunger and fear that drew them there sharply. How long is the wait for the train? she asked. The darkness lightened. They were at the railway yard in Ixtepec and she was standing next to the tracks. The grey stones lay beneath her feet. The town's detritus was mixed among them: scattered papers, plastic bags, cigarette butts, chewing gum, rotting bits of food. He saw the body of a man on the metal rails. A frozen look of terror in the man's unseeing eyes. Is it someone we know? she asked.

It's midmorning and someone yells out, Tierra Blanca.

There's a shelter in this town, Pedro says, we'll get off here for a day or two.

Emilio wishes Rigoberto safe journey to North Carolina and follows Pedro toward the ladder. He helps Matilde to the small metal area between two cars and the four jump off the train, one at a time, along with several other migrants, once the Beast has slowed inside the perimeter of the town. They follow a group of backpacked men who seem to know where they are going, and in twenty minutes they find Albergue Decanal Guadalupano on Aldama Street.

The four write their names in the shelter's ledger: Pedro Gaitán García, Matilde Ramírez Sánchez, Emilio Ramos Matias, and William Gutiérrez Campos. Afterward they join the other new arrivals for a hot meal of beans and soup in the large dining area.

It is this generosity in the midst of the unknown, alongside our disquiet, and the high stone walls of safety, Emilio thinks, that I will remember in the future when I'm home.

The father enters the lunchroom to welcome and bless them. He goes table to table and listens as the men describe the attack by the Zetas and the taking of more than sixty people from La Bestia. When the father reaches their group, Pedro tells him of the kidnapping of their companion, Jonatan Ildefonso Orellana Mejía, and of the murders of the two others.

Someone ought to give them a proper burial, Father, Pedro says. It's a half-day south of here.

The volunteer accompanying the priest writes down the details in his notebook, and the father promises he will notify the humanitarian groups and report it to the newspapers. People are scared now to publish anything of this nature, the father says, several journalists have disappeared, and others have been threatened. We continue to pray, brother, we continue the fight for justice. We pray for you and your missing friend, and for Mexico and Honduras and Guatemala.

Emilio showers after the meal and it is a small pleasure he has learned to appreciate each time: to remove the grime is glorious, and in small things and small ways his suffering is alleviated. He runs his tongue over his clean teeth and gums and he wishes for a moment the shelter provided its guests with dental floss, it's been weeks since I've flossed, he thinks, and he realizes immediately how ridiculous that sounds here and now. A volunteer provided them clean clothes and they wash their dirty ones in the concrete basins and hang them up outside to dry.

Pedro says that they'll stay one extra night, but it's better to keep going toward the capital, muchachos. We have not come this far to turn back now, we must give it our best, he repeats, his continual mantra. We put our faith in God. Only He is our guide.

Emilio reaches into the pocket of the borrowed jeans for the stone he has placed there. He knows that despite and perhaps because of everything they have endured he must keep going, he must stay with her. Yes, he says.

He looks at Matilde, who had wanted to stay at least three nights in the shelter but says okay, and then at William, who nods his assent and follows Pedro without question.

In Mexico City we'll relax, maybe even have a beer, Pedro says, as if to cheer himself.

And although they are determined to continue north, they feel the defeat and pain and sorrow that accompanies them now in Jonatan's absence.

It is safer to return to your countries, the father had warned them, like all the previous fathers. The cartels have power because they have the money, and our national institutions are in disarray. It is only more dangerous for the undocumented, brothers.

But the migrants cannot be discouraged. I'd rather die on the road in my attempt for something better, they say, than starve or be killed at home.

Emilio finds two unoccupied beds on one of the bunk beds after dinner. He tells Matilde to take the top one and he'll sleep down below. William has found another open bunk with Pedro. Goodnight, he whispers to her.

Sleep well, she says.

Mom, I can't move. At the back of my legs and the bottom of my arms, a trenchant kind of fatigue. A paralysis has set in to the deepest muscles and they don't respond, contract, or loosen.

Son, a certain knowledge awaits you.

I'm tired inside my bones.

Son, it lies quietly at the back of the mind. Behold the occipital.

Mother, your voice in the darkness

. . .

Mother, the natural visions

. . .

We saw a murmuration in the corn field and its staggering beauty was absolute.

They remain inside the high walls of the shelter the next day. They rest and eat and aid with chores and exchange stories and precautionary tales with the other migrants who are passing through. They consult the maps on the wall to determine their best route.

Matilde cleans one of the dormitories and Emilio has just finished helping dig a trench for new water and sewage pipes with several volunteers behind the main building.

He is tired after the exertion and joins a small group of young Guatemalans in the shade of the patio. He listens while a laborer from Antigua recounts a story he heard a few days ago in another shelter.

There were seventy-two, the young laborer says. Ecuadorans, Salvadorans, Hondurans, Brazilians, Cubans, and an Indian from Asia! They had paid their coyotes at least six thousand apiece to ride in private trucks the easy way and they almost made it to the line, but then it wasn't easy. Eighty kilometers from the border armed men forced the lorries off the road and took them to a ranch in San Fernando, in Tamaulipas. The assailants took the women inside a warehouse and the men's hands and feet were tied up and they were made to lie on the ground. No one knows why the assailants did what they did after that. Why they didn't seek the usual payout from families. They brought the girls outside after they had used them and told them to lie next to the men. Then they shot every last one. An Ecuadoran got a bullet in the mouth but he played dead and walked to the highway after the assailants took off and the army found him. At first the soldiers didn't believe the Ecuadoran, but when they discovered the massacre even the newspapers had to report the story because it was such a big scandal. The national police don't go into that state anymore, the Señores control the territory completely, so I'm telling you to stay out of Tamaulipas when you get into the northern states close to the border. Cross over in Sonora.

Emilio closes his eyes to the bright shade beneath the awning and to the Guatemalan's story. He's glad Matilde didn't hear it. He thinks about Jonatan and sees again the men with their black ski masks and military costumes and tennis shoes on their feet; the contingent of local policemen who aided them; the fat boss in his bright yellow polo shirt, pressed blue jeans, reflective sunglasses, and his cowboy boots. He feels the tension he always carries as it increases its force. It's been fifteen days since I left Todos Santos, and in those fifteen nothing is the same, he thinks.

I can't do it, Pedro, Matilde says as they ready to leave the shelter after breakfast in the morning. I thought I could, but I can't.

We must put our best foot forward. We must get out of the south to the capital. We are close now.

Emilio stands next to Matilde and watches her. He knows what she will do for he has learned her fortitude, and the four leave a few minutes later. It is his own mantra now, joined with the *can I ever get it all back*: forward going with her.

They wait behind some bushes near the tracks for several hours until they finally hear the train horn and Pedro says to run. The four dash toward the rails and two policemen spot them, but they manage to climb aboard the moving train before the police can intercept them. They are northward bound again. This cargo train has no hoppers and so they ride on top in the wind and with the sun on them.

The Beast rushes by fields of corn and here the mosquitoes swarm worse than ever. They are batting their hands and faces and arms in each town when the train slows and the mosquitoes blackly surround them. Their faces are soon marked with red bites and Emilio tells Matilde she looks like she has the chicken pox. He is making light of it like Jonatan would, and she makes a face at him, because for whatever reason the mosquitoes bite her more than they do him. The train heads toward Orizaba, climbs slowly into the colder regions. In the late afternoon they see Mexico's tallest mountain, Pico de Orizaba, grandiose and snow-covered, above the large valley.

We'll get off and get something to eat, Pedro says.

They are hungry again, the cold is settling into their bodies, and Emilio is glad they will get down from the train for a respite. The four have been riding silently for hours, enduring the late morning, the long afternoon.

Pedro and William head into town to find a store and purchase tortillas and cheese with their remaining seventy-five pesos as soon as they jump off the train. He and Matilde remain alongside the tracks, waiting with a dozen other migrants. The temperature has dropped precipitously and she is trembling and says she didn't think it would be so much cooler here than it was in Chiapas and Oaxaca.

He puts his arm around her to warm her and she leans into his body. She has the hood of her sweatshirt pulled tightly around her face, as she usually does, covering her long hair.

I want to know something, Emilio, she says.

What?

How it happened.

How what happened?

You lived there your whole life, right, so how did they know?

It's a long story, he says, for another day.

I want to understand you better, she says.

She looks up at him, and he can see she is tired and the fear is in her dark eyes and she tightens and closes them slightly, and the sadness. Her mouth is tensed, everything pulled in toward the back of her countenance by the continual apprehension while they travel. By the losses.

It was bad luck, he says. I was on my way home from a party when the car in front of us on the freeway hit the car ahead of it and my friend from school who was driving swerved and didn't hit anybody, but the guy behind us slammed the bumper and we all pulled over to the side. The police arrived quickly. It was obvious who had caused the accident, but the policemen asked all of us for our IDs since it looked like a drunk-driving incident and then because of more bad luck—

More?

Police in my town don't inform on immigrants, it's a sanctuary city, and anyway immigration is civil not criminal law, but I wasn't in Berkeley that day, and because I didn't have ID they took me in.

He looks up at the white snowy peak of the volcano in the distance.

The police figured out I was undocumented and they called the migra. The migra came and took me to a detention center.

I'm sorry, she says.

My friend hadn't even been drinking, and I'd only had one beer.

He looks back at her.

Once they arrested me there was nothing anyone in my family could do, not even the attorney my mom hired. I lost my job; I missed all my classes. After a month in jail I realized that sooner or later the government would deport me, so I decided to take matters into my own hands. I didn't ask anyone for advice. I didn't tell anyone in my family. I signed the form the head of the detention center assured me would free me. He expedited my removal after that and they sent me to Guatemala ten days later.

Why would you do that?

Because I couldn't take it anymore, he says, not looking at her again but at the immense mountain. Because they would have held me in that jail for years like the fifteen guys I shared a room with: waiting, worrying, helpless, and losing everything. I thought about it and I carefully considered my options and I decided to let them send me back and that I would reenter on my own. Return to the life I'd always had.

You didn't deserve that, she says.

He looks down at her and sees again her kindness, her sorrow, her beautiful dark eyes and full mouth. The raised red marks from the insect bites on her skin.

I got depressed, he says. They confiscated all my personal belongings when I got there and made me wear an orange jumpsuit like the other inmates. We had to wake up when the guards told us, eat what they gave us, go to sleep at lights out, line up for bed counts three to four times a day when they called us by our number. They let us outside only two hours a day. When one of my roommates got sent up to solitary for a week, I decided I had to get out of there. But the final humiliation came after I'd hoped to be done with all of it.

He laughs.

There were twenty of us waiting on the tarmac to board the airplane, mostly middle-aged guys who had worked construction, or as gardeners or cooks, for decades, and most with American kids and wives they were leaving behind. Before they let us board the chartered flight, the officers handcuffed our wrists and bound our ankles with leg irons. They said they couldn't free us until our feet touched the ground of our own country. That it was government protocol. So I arrived to Guatemala City in chains.

He takes his arm from around Matilde and pulls the white stone out of his pocket.

Your American friends, your girlfriend, no one could help you?

No.

He puts the stone back in his pocket. I lost everything and I don't know if I will get it back, he says.

He feels Matilde place her hand on the top of the hand he sheathed in the front pocket of his jeans, the one that worries the stone again.

Maybe I made a mistake signing that paper. The warden assured me it would free me, he said it was the only way, and I just wanted out of there. I don't know. Now I only want to see my family again. I want to return to school. Maybe I can get my job back.

You'll make it, she says. I have a good feeling.

And then as usual he can feel their invisible electric exchange, she to him and he to her: the mutual force of their attraction. He puts his arm around her again and pulls her into his body to warm her. Perhaps I was reckless and stupid, he thinks, but together we will see it through.

Pedro and William return with a bag of food and another filled with used clothing that Pedro tells them an old man handed to him as he was buying the tortillas. We'll need these for the ascent into the mountains, he says, as he pulls three sweaters out of the bag, where it will get even colder.

Matilde puts an old blue sweater on top of her hooded sweatshirt and William says he is fine and that Emilio and Pedro should use the remaining two.

I don't get cold, he says.

Are you sure? Pedro says. His cough is almost but not entirely gone.

Yes, William says, and he returns to his usual silence.

When night comes on, the train is still at the station. They sleep exposed near the tracks as the temperature continues to drop. The men take turns keeping vigil. Matilde sleeps on Emilio's legs while he also falls asleep, shivering, in the hours before dawn.

Jonatan said: I seek what I cannot find.

They took us to a deserted house and put us into a large room and bound our hands. They didn't feed us or give us water and they beat us and some perished because they were already very tired and dehydrated. I told them I didn't have anything. That I was a combi driver from Tegucigalpa with no relatives in USA.

They transferred me after that to a smaller room and they beat me again with their guns. They said, Are you sure, asshole, you don't have a phone number for Texas or Los Angeles?

I told them once more that I drove a bus in the Honduran capital and they continued hitting me all over my body and because my no's did not become yeses they concluded, eventually, that I was cargo with no exchange value: something that could not be sold back to its family for thousands of dollars.

When I had no recognizable face and my teeth were gone, my eyes, they announced that they were going to throw a party and have some fun. They turned on a music player and the Mexican norteña music everyone in this country loves so well played loudly and they covered my mouth with duct tape and strung me up by my feet. I could not see because blind, or speak because gagged, but I heard the loud music and the drunken, rowdy, laughing men. One of them held my naked swinging body from behind and steadied me. I was motionless, hanged, and a second man said, Now watch the little piggy squirm, and he grabbed me by my testicles. He began to cut with a small knife. And the little bit of life left in me surged and I twisted this way and that but he took everything.

I saw myself then suspended like an animal at a slaughterhouse. The man with the small knife resumed getting high and laughing with the others and when he returned to my side he began to cut the skin where my neck met my shoulder. Did I stay to watch it? I didn't stay. This has become a Godforsaken place with unsanctioned men whose business is to take a man, any man—Salvadoran, Honduran, Guatemalan, Mexican—and undo him for profit or at a loss. No love among us.

Tell my mother and my wife: Jonatan is okay.

Yet I confess, brother, I am uncertain when I might return to them. For now I remain here with the man who unmade me. I am his nightmares. One day he too will become victim to a cartel sicario for all they that take the sword shall perish with it, *and afterward he will join me in this loud parade of the infernal dead. We wait in Mexico and I am hopeful the passage of days will diminish our outrage further. Then I might return to Tegus, to my wife and child and my old mother, and you can find me there in a small garden next to an evergreen and resting finally in that place in peace.*

Emilio awakens when the train's engine starts up loudly. They stand and run to grab it. Matilde goes first while Pedro yells get on, get on. She boards with relative ease and as Pedro reaches for the ladder his outer foot slips and Matilde watches him and a look of horror crosses her face. She is yelling hold on, hold on, while the suction of the wheels pulls Pedro's left leg and he panics but with the help of another migrant he manages to pull himself on board. William swings up next, then Emilio, and they find enough space by the back of a wagon for all four of them. Someone left an old blanket and they are grateful for it riding down below with some protection from the wind at the end of a hopper and to have a cover for their bodies.

The train blows its horn and slows as they pass through another small town. A group of boys run out of their trackside shanties and several of the migrants on the tops of the train stand up in anticipation of shared food or water. Down below a few men hold their arms out at the ready to catch anything the boys might share.

The boys run closer to the tracks and begin to hurl rocks and insults.

Go back to your countries, one yells, as he throws a large stone at a boxcar.

187

Stay out of Mexico, another yells, you bring all the problems here.

The rocks hit the sides of the steel cars and one lands beside them on the hopper.

Dirty scum! a third boy says. Dirty migrants.

Pedro picks up the small rock that landed next to him. Such children, he says.

The train pulls out of the town and leaves the rock throwers behind.

The temperature has fallen and the four huddle together to stay warm. The train passes through miles of fields of radishes, corn, and lettuces and their variations in green. At moments Emilio thinks about Jonatan, about his last glimpse of his tall dark head above the other migrants as he stumbled toward the ladder. He wonders where he is; he wishes he could do something for him. Matilde holds the old blue sweater close to her thin body and the hood of her grey sweatshirt is tied closely around her face; together they watch the changing scenery as the train begins ascending higher into the mountains. They doze and the train cars creak and clang.

A Nicaraguan called Miguel who has recently joined them at the end of the hopper yells out, There he is!, as they leave another town, and they turn their eyes to see the immense white statue of Christ the Redeemer on a nearby mountaintop. Many of the riders genuflect, honoring and revering the One who suffered before them and for them and who will, they hope, protect and guide them. Please, Señor, they say out loud as they pray. Matilde makes the sign of the cross on her body and Pedro, William, and

Miguel also form the symbol with their right hands. Emilio watches but keeps both his hands in his pockets, the thumb and index finger of his right pressed around his talisman.

We are climbing the Cumbres de Acultzingo and will arrive to the tunnels soon, Pedro says. There are more than thirty of them, each one named for a state in Mexico. Some are short and fast, and others long, and they are dark inside, but the trains go through them quickly, muchachos. After that, we finally arrive to the capital!

The way now is steep. They are high in the mountains and they enter the first tunnel: it is pitch-black and they travel through it in a few minutes. The train rushes to the next one and then the next. Sometimes the tail of the Beast has not left one tunnel behind before its engine enters another. Black and loud and smoke-filled; the darkness for short or long periods, then the light of day. Emilio cannot see his hand in front of his face, then he sees it, then it vanishes once more. The train continues its climb, the air becomes progressively colder. They cling to the old blanket; their faces are grey and black soot runs from their noses.

Now they have entered the tenth and the end of the tunnel cannot be seen. Emilio has his arms around Matilde's shoulders and because the smoke in this tunnel is strong and noxious, they have covered their mouths with their sweaters and they breathe through the fabric as the engine emits more smoke and fills up the black passageway. It's getting more difficult to breathe, Emilio, he hears her say. Then they move into the clear air of the day and she inhales deeply.

The Beast now enters the longest one, the fifteenth. It continues moving quickly for a time and then begins to decelerate: smoke fills up the tunnel as the train slows. It finally comes to a full stop in the darkness. The walls of the tunnel are close and there is no space next to the tracks to get down or walk that Emilio can ascertain. I can't breathe, he thinks, as the minutes begin to pass in the cold and black smoke and the blackness is ugly and he is a body but he cannot see where it begins or ends or his hands and we could asphyxiate and perish like stray dogs at a kill shelter, he thinks. They wait quietly. No one says very much, afraid to use up more oxygen talking. Matilde reaches for his dark hand and she holds it.

What is it? What could it be? Miguel's voice says into the darkness.

There is no way for the migrants to know the answer. Perhaps the engine overheated on the climb?

As the minutes slowly pass fear rises in the bodies of all the travelers. They try and nap in the black smoke, but it is more and more difficult to breathe easily. The passengers are coughing in the tunnel and Miguel is talking to God and coughing, saying the tunnels are worse than he thought they would be. Matilde has pressed her face into Emilio's chest. They are trying to remain still, to breathe shallowly, they continue to use their sweaters and shirts as filters for the air. Pedro has said this happens sometimes, remain calm, muchachos. They shiver; they try to breathe. We'll get going soon, it always does, he says. He is coughing as if he is sick again.

After more than a half hour has passed, Miguel stands and says he can't take any more of this black smoke. Why won't it start up and move us out of here? I'll walk, he says to them, and jump back on on the outside. Pedro tells him that surely, any moment, it will begin moving again, that this happens sometimes, that he should stay with them. It's not a good idea, man, you'll be all right, breathe through your shirt, Pedro says between small fits of coughing. Lie down on the metal landing and think about a place in your village that is quiet and green and brings you ease.

I can't breathe, Miguel says from the darkness, I can't take it anymore. He jumps down. They hear his feet hitting the rocks and running along. Pedro is coughing nonstop now.

A quarter of an hour or so later the train's engine starts up and anticipation lifts around them. The cars slowly begin to move and the smoke is lessened.somewhat by the movement and it seems like light will arrive soon and the fresh air of the day. They think they hear an anguished yell. Miguel? Matilde says. In another twenty minutes the train pulls out of the tunnel and into the sun-light and if I believed in God I could not give Him more of my thanks right now, Emilio thinks, as he takes in large gulps of cold clean air.

Her face is covered in black soot.

You look like you have been dipped into a pot of black ink, he jokes.

But Matilde is distraught and can't be distracted. What do you think happened to the Nicaraguan? she asks.

I don't know.

Emilio, every day I ask myself: What did we do to deserve this?

He has no answer to give her; he pulls her into his arms tighter and holds her as the train continues along its route.

The sun sets and it is dark inside and outside of the tunnels now and colder, but the train doesn't stop again; it moves through tunnel after tunnel, from black to blacker.

Sleep if you can, he tells her.

They are dozing and he tries to warm her and he wonders if she is thinking of her children and he is trying not to think of the Nicaraguan, of Jonatan, of how many tunnels remain, of the long night still ahead of them, of the nights after that until they reach the border.

He hears Pedro coughing in his sleep.

When they pass through a small town he looks over at William and sees in the dim light that he is not sleeping either but staring intently up at the stars.

I wanted to ask you so many times, Emilio says, breaking a long silence, why you left Honduras, why you are going to the North.

William lowers his gaze from the sky and just before he closes his eyes, thereby curtailing further conversation, offers only one word in response: necessity.

Miguel was talking to him. He was saying: Because even from this side, we would like it known.

I couldn't take it anymore: the smoke, the dark, and I couldn't breathe. I'm tired and the trip has been lengthy and along every step there has been a policeman or a gang member to make it more difficult. I was sure I would make it to the North because it was my dream, like this dream you are having now, but a good one, you understand, to have money and security and feed my children and have a better future. But I couldn't breathe and I have always been afraid of enclosed spaces, since I was young boy. I need to be outside with the sky and the wind and the stars and trees and so I didn't in fact mind traveling on the Beast because in the open air I was, despite everything, happier.

Therefore, I jumped down. And below I could breathe a little easier and I began walking on the rocks. There was very little space between the train and the tunnel walls and I couldn't even see my feet at the end of my legs. I only wanted to get out of the tunnel and into the open air. I was walking and moving slowly over stones and trying to make my way in a straight line, but once I left the train behind me I couldn't see the end of the tunnel, the light, or my body, and so when the Beast started up again with her loud rumble of engine and wheels and began moving toward me there was very little room for me at the side of the track but I was okay because the train had its three lights illuminated and I could see it approach, I could finally see my feet. I held myself to the wall and waited. There was so little room and the train began roar-

ing by me; there was nothing to hold on to but it was okay and I was praying to God, help me Señor, and everything was okay, and I was pressing myself back into the tunnel's wall and praying and saying to myself, just a little bit longer, Miguel, maybe five more minutes before the train has passed and then you'll walk out of here and catch the next one. I was holding on to nothing and leaning as heavily with my back and thighs into the tunnel wall as I could to resist the increasing suction of the locomotive. But the Beast began tugging on me strongly, car after car, pulling me toward her like a violent lover, and although I was resisting and leaning away, she was dominant and took me. I could not stop her. Then light and it was in me. And although I didn't feel the cleave of the metal wheels, I do now feel a longing for something which is impossible to realize. No Americandream. I seek myself here in this tunnel, the longest one: El Mexicano.

But please tell me, friend, how does a man go home again, how can he arrive without his feet and his legs?

Emilio had dozed for a few hours and now wakes with the sunlight on him. The sun rises. The four sleep inside an open boxcar filled with lumber which they'd climbed into during the night. She lies between his legs and sleeps and he looks down at her soot-covered and bite-marked visage, her black lashes lying coldly on her gaunt cheeks, and he thinks how before this journey they both led such different lives. And then the old outrage rises in him again: that he was barred from his home and forbidden reentry; that he was jailed like a criminal; that his lawyer could do nothing to help him even though the rest of his family members have legal status. And then the fear and humiliation he has lived with since his parents told him at sixteen that he wasn't a citizen and that he would always have to be cautious. And after that (looking at the girl) a surging tenderness, his determination, his bitter gall. He sees large green spiky cacti and a desiccated valley and two great pyramids rising from the landscape beyond—the ancient remains of Teotihuacán.

He wakes her up to see it. Her eyes are red and dull. Pedro and William are stretched out, dozing on their backs on planks of wood.

Look, he says, you will see one of the wonders of the world.

She looks out at the majestic temples and then back at him. He has his arms around her and she presses closer into his chest and he feels that strange sense of ease he always feels when she is near, and this new love.

It's the place of the gods, he says. It was the largest city in Pre-Colombian America. It existed before the Aztecs or the Maya, it was built more than two thousand years ago.

How do you know so much about it? she asks.

I took a history course about Mesoamerica at the university, he says, and he laughs at how absurd that sounds sitting on a pile of lumber and riding on the top of a train like a vagrant.

But I never thought to see it for the first time from a cargo train with a pretty girl from the capital of Honduras and as dirty as I've ever been in my life.

Life is crazy, she says, and she laughs also.

Pedro awakens and he nudges William to wake up.

Mexico City is a dangerous transit stop, Pedro says, the police look for migrants everywhere. We'll hop off before Lechería and walk in. We're getting close now, the pyramids are only fifty kilometers from the city.

The train slowly advances. Emilio sees housing developments, signs for tobacco and women's face cream. They gather their things. They share the last remnants of their food and get ready to jump off the train and run. The metropolis approaches them as they approach it, massive and alive.

We're finally out of the south, he thinks.

The Desert

May 31, 2012

The world is like the impression left by the telling of a story.

Yogavāsiṣṭha

They are on the bus. Small overhead televisions play loudly and the air conditioning blasts coldly. Matilde sits next to a window and stares out of it. Emilio sits behind her in an aisle seat looking at the other passengers and keeping his eye on her and on Juan.

He is feeling optimistic and it is the first such feeling since the kidnapping by the Zetas on the train eight days ago. He is happy to be on a clean coach bus and the blisters on his feet are slowly beginning to heal, his ankle is no longer so swollen. They bought clean shirts and new backpacks and new jeans for the both of them, and with a certain hopefulness, he even purchased another journal and pen. He knows she worries about Pedro and William, who have been riding the trains from Mexico City for at least half a day already, but Pedro assured her that they would be fine and they would see each other in El Sásabe in three days. God willing, Matilde had said.

She and Emilio are together.

He paid for their tickets and for Juan, their guide. He told his mother about Matilde and his friends when he phoned her, and his mother was crying hysterically, Son Son Son, I thought you were dead, we thought you had died, your poor Aunt Lourdes has been out of her mind with worry. Why didn't you ask me for money? I would have borrowed if necessary, Susana and Peter would have helped me. I would have done anything. Why didn't you tell me? I haven't slept and I can't eat since the nineteen days ago when you went missing from Todos Santos. Son, Son, Son, my God, my God, I thought you had been killed, Aunt Lourdes thought you were kidnapped by a gang. Son, my Son, thank God, thank God, you are okay. Thank God you are alive.

And he also cried on the telephone, exhausted from running for the past ten miles and hiding and dodging the police. They had spent the night sleeping in a pickup truck on a small residential street, the men taking turns to keep watch until first light. It was obvious to any who saw them from their dirty faces and their stink that they were migrants on the run.

They found a small store in the early morning and Pedro bought a liter of orange Fanta and some chips with their remaining Mexican pesos. Emilio thought the cold sweet soda was the best thing he had ever tasted. They waited in front of a pay telephone store until it opened and then he called his mother collect in Berkeley and her: Son, Son, Son, my God, I thought you were dead.

His mother wired three hundred dollars immediately: enough for food and to get them into a motel for a few nights. Emilio stood in line at the Western Union with his black hands and black face and soiled fetid clothing, and the three waited for him outside in the street. He couldn't help but notice how the other customers and the agent who finally assisted him looked at him with mostly unveiled disgust and disdain.

Cash in hand, they ate a quick snack at an outdoor market and bought clean shirts and underwear and cheap track pants and looked for a motel and checked in. They let Matilde shower first and they didn't even sit on the beds while they each awaited their turns because they were so dirty.

A bath made them all new.

William accompanied Emilio to find a pharmacy to buy toothbrushes, aspirin and antibiotic ointment for their feet and faces, and cough medicine for Pedro. The other two remained in the motel resting on the beds and watching TV and he promised to bring a hot meal for their dinner.

When they exited the pharmacy with their purchases, Emilio asked William what he was in the mood for.

Whatever you want to eat is okay with me, William said.

You don't have a preference?

No.

More sweet rolls from a street vendor? Emilio said to make light of things while they walked along the busy crowded sidewalk of the capital.

William shook his head.

They found a pizza place near the motel and ordered two larges. I've been dreaming about pizza for weeks, Emilio thought. They sat at one of the red plastic tables inside the restaurant and drank a Coke while they awaited their order. Mexican rock music played loudly. William sat across from him and was silent as usual and Emilio thought how strange it was that even now he knew so little about him. William at least looked more comfortable in a new tee shirt and cleaned up.

How are you feeling? Emilio asked.

Good.

Do you miss home much?

No.

You miss your parents? Or a girlfriend? Emilio smiles.

No.

I'm twenty-one, but you're younger than me, right?

Eighteen.

Are you still in high school?

No.

Did you work somewhere?

No.

No? What did you do back home?

Nothing.

Nothing?

Pretty much.

You have relatives in the North you'll stay with?

One brother.

Where does he live?

I haven't talked to him since I was five so, excuse me, William said, I need to use the toilet. He stood up and went in search of the bathroom.

They left the restaurant with the two large pizzas as soon as William returned.

In the motel, the four sat on the beds and watched television and ate fast food until their bellies were filled and they relaxed. She lay next to him, and Pedro and William shared the other bed.

I like this room, Pedro said, patting his stomach, more comfortable and talkative now that the medicine had taken effect. His cough was almost gone again.

The next morning, Emilio called his mother for the second time. She had spoken to neighbors and friends at the bakery and found him a guide in the capital, she said. Luisa insisted he was trustworthy and reliable, his name is Chaco. Do you need any more money? Luisa said he successfully crossed three of her nephews last year. Call Chaco now and organize the details, he's expecting to hear from you.

There are multiple checkpoints between the capital and the border, but my colleague will go with you and the new IDs will make it no problem, Chaco said. He will find you tomorrow at your motel to get your pictures. I'll meet you in El Sásabe in three days for my next tour. Tell your friends it's two thousand a piece from the line. For you and the girl, three thousand five hundred a person, your mother already arranged to give me seven hundred up front. Three tries included for that price.

Emilio returned to the motel from the telephone cabina and told them the price and that he'd pay the extra cost for her to go with him on the bus.

Neither Matilde nor Pedro argued with him. Don't worry about us, it's easier from here, Pedro said to Matilde when she said it might not be safe for them on the trains either.

Emilio brought back hamburgers and french fries for their lunch and they sat in the room on the beds and watched more television. They were all contented to eat and rest and watch. Even William smiled at the dumb Mexican comedy that played, laughed a little bit when the fat actor was begging a beautiful woman on his knees to please let him kiss her.

We must keep up our spirits, Pedro would start saying if he saw one of them looking sad or worried, we have come so far, muchachos.

That night as the other two slept and Pedro snored softly, Emilio and Matilde held hands under the cover of darkness. Emilio rubbed his thumb inside the palm of Matilde's hand, and he remembered how his mother had told him that morning on the telephone that Antonia was out of her mind with worry.

Son, I know you haven't spoken in months, but I felt the need to let her know you were okay, she begged me to have you call her. But I am not ready, he thought, to speak with Antonia. The old Emilio still loved her: her lithe strong body and light-brown hair and the white stone she gave him, which he was convinced more and more, protected him. But she was another girl for another boy because now there was only Matilde who in the past day had begun to relax a little, she was eating more, and she looked rested and lovelier. Still, he wondered, he couldn't seem to help himself, what Antonia might be doing now. Drinking a latte at Café Strada and studying for a final exam? Or resting from a five-mile run in the hills behind campus in the late afternoon? She could be planning for the summer courses she would take, the internship she had applied for. Maybe she had met someone else by now, as he had. He caressed Matilde's fingers, and as he began to lose consciousness he thought about the waning moon in the sky, which he couldn't see tonight because of the walls, the ceiling.

Pedro and William departed for the train depot after a hearty breakfast. They carried a black backpack and in it provisions for the journey: bread, cheese, cookies, water bottles, an extra pair of socks, some aspirin, their toothbrushes, and the cough medicine in case Pedro needed it again. They had forty dollars hidden in their shoes. Matilde was visibly worried. You'll be okay? she said to Pedro again.

We'll see you in three days.

She hugged Pedro and then William. William looked unhappy as always, and scared, but he continued to put his faith in Pedro to take him all the way up.

God willing, Matilde said.

In an hour there was a knock on the door and Emilio asked who it was (the winch working as always, gripping and tightening inside him), and a voice said Chaco sent me. Emilio opened the door to a young, clean-cut guy in his twenties in dark, pressed blue jeans and a button-down shirt.

Good morning, I'm Juan.

He had a camera, and he said he would take their photographs and tomorrow he'd give them their Mexican identity cards to use when the bus was stopped and revised at the military checkpoints.

He told Matilde to say she lived in the capital and that her name was Ximena González Prieta if questioned. You are Miguel Ángel del Río from a small village in Oaxaca called Agua del Pino. She and I will say we are married. Don't talk too much, he said to her, your accent is noticeably catracho, and you sound half-American plus you're Indian-looking so keep quiet. All right?

They made plans to meet at a restaurant by the bus station. Dress cleanly, neatly, wear a little makeup, he said to Matilde. He told Emilio to slick back his hair.

Juan took their photographs and he departed.

It was eleven o'clock and Emilio was sitting on the bed again and leaning against the headboard. She sat next to him and they watched a New York police show dubbed into Spanish.

They were alone and they had never, since they'd met over two weeks ago, been together in a private room, clean and sated and rested, and for the moment, unafraid.

In the morning they would leave on the last leg of their journey. He was afraid for tomorrow and yet as he felt her body against his keenly, electrically, as he always did, he started to become aroused. She twisted her hair with her index and middle fingers while they watched the police show, a Mexican talk show, a game show, and the day passed.

At two o'clock he went outside and bought women's makeup from a department store and a blouse for her and a new shirt for him and some pomade, and then finally tacos and Cokes from a street vendor and he returned with their fare. She had not left the room since they arrived, she said she didn't want to go out, buy me whatever you think will look good, black kohl pencil and black mascara.

They were sitting on the bed now and eating their repast.

I got so hungry again, she said, these are delicious. She took another bite of her taco. Their food is good, but I don't trust them, she said.

He knew she was thinking of their guide.

It's better Juan is with us.

Everything they've done to us, she said. When foreigners come to Honduras we are hospitable. Here they treat us like dogs.

He is a colleague of Chaco's and he'll take care of us. I grew up with a lot of Mexicans so I know they're not all bad.

They finished their lunch. They watched more television. She fell asleep and he couldn't sleep. He leaned against the headboard and she lay supine between his legs now. When she finally awoke it was darker in the room and the noise of the capital was loud outside the windows. He took her hand and although she didn't let go of his hand he could feel she was anxious.

Matilde, you ought to call your mother, you should speak with your children. I have some money left on the calling card and we could go to the cabina around the corner.

No. No, not yet. I can't talk to them yet. In United States, later, after we arrive I'll call them. Then I'll have something good to say to them. It's better not to talk too much now.

They were silent after that. He focused on the TV show and tried to distract himself. I want to lie next to her, touch her day and night, he thought.

Matilde, what was your dream? he asked during a long commercial break. As a child. What did you think about for your future?

Me?

What did you imagine?

That was a long time ago.

You're too old to remember? he joked.

I know it sounds stupid, but I wanted to study the birds, she finally said. When I was a girl my father kept over a dozen on the garden patio. Later I thought maybe I'd become a secretary, but instead I became a seamstress at a tee shirt factory.

Why didn't you study?

Many of the teachers never showed up to class at the high school I attended, or they would go on strike for weeks at a time, and sometimes they were brutal. Then I met Raúl and my son was born.

They were quiet again and the commercials finished and a soap opera began.

Do you know William from home? he asked, bored by the drama, absorbed by his attraction to this girl.

I only know that he lives a few houses away from Pedro in the same colonia.

I tried to talk to him yesterday, but he doesn't say much.

He too has learned our habit of silence.

Do you know why he's going up?

Pedro only told me they went to his house.

Who did?

The Mara Salvatrucha. The leaders of the clica in his neighborhood gave the ultimatum: join or die. The usual. His mother called Pedro that night and begged him to take William to an older half-brother. The 18th Street controls mine, and they are just as bad.

They watched another television show. He dozed and then woke up. He was restless and nervous and broke the long silence again between them.

Matilde.

Yes?

Have you healed?

He could feel the muscles pull up her body and tighten along her legs, her arms.

I want to kiss you, he said.

She sat up now and pulled away from him to look at him in the dimness of the room.

Since that moment at the shelter in Tecún Umán when I found you again. I want to hold you and take care of you.

She only stared at him. Began to twist and pull her long dark hair with the dyed blond pieces.

Can you feel it? he said, for he couldn't stop talking now. I want so much to kiss you, can I kiss you? Perhaps you are not ready and perhaps I'm crazy, but it's something inside me, he said, and he gently took hold of the hand that pulled on her hair. The blue light and noise from the television screen filled the room and his longing filled up inside him, the long journey that bound them, the trepidation and the unknown that awaited them.

What about your girlfriend?

I don't know the future, I only know what I feel right now. I want to be near you. To adore you.

Emilio, she said, I'm not good anymore. And she began to cry.

Once she had begun, she continued for a long time in the blue light, in the dark-blue shadows. Emilio thought perhaps she wouldn't stop, that the tears had filled up in her to such a degree she would be the crier for eternity, the lady who is perpetually weeping. He held her and the night descended down fully on them and the corners of the room were now almost black and eventually the storm passed. She was quiet, exhausted against him. She released his hand. He couldn't see her face, but he felt her muscles relax.

It hurts in my heart, she said into the room.

He knew it wasn't right, that she was grieving, but his mounting desire for her pulsed through him again and he imagined seeing her beautiful body and touching her breasts and pleasing her and moving inside her, becoming, if only for a moment, part of her. I need her, he thought, and this need is beyond anything I have ever known.

I must leave you to your girlfriend, she said. We are transients. We are only passing through. Our paths have crossed, but only God decides.

Can I hold you while we sleep?

She told him that he could and he turned off the television. He wrapped his arms around her waist in the dark and pressed into her body and he was, in this way, appeased.

In the morning he woke up before she did with his hard cock pressed into her ass, and for a moment he thought only of what he could say to make her desire him and then he felt ashamed.

He went into the bathroom and masturbated and then urinated. He looked into the mirror as he washed his hands and saw a man who was new to him: the dark-brown eyes looking back from the now darker brown and leaner face; the strain apparent in the small contractions of the small muscles around his eyes and mouth; the new creases on this brow; the longer unruly black hair. I can see him, he thought, a different man.

He woke her and they showered and dressed. She lined her eyes in black and put her hair up, she donned the pretty casual blouse he purchased for her yesterday. She looked like any young woman leaving her house to go to work in the morning. His hair was slicked back on his head like he sometimes used to wear it when going to a party. They exited the building; it was her first time outside in three days. They found a stand and ordered freshly squeezed orange juice and a breakfast bread. He did all the talking for them and she didn't look anyone in the eye. They met Juan at the designated restaurant and he gave them their IDs and the three boarded the bus within the hour.

They are moving northward now. A movie plays on the small televisions above their seats and the passengers laugh at the antics of a Mexican comedy.

The bus slows for the first military control after they pass the capital limits. Matilde looks back at Emilio and Juan grabs her hand to get her attention and holds it, caresses it, and Emilio feels a surge of jealousy rise steeply in his body even though he knows Juan is probably only doing it to keep up appearances. A soldier gets on the bus in army fatigues and walks down the center aisle looking at each passenger (but I would stop Juan if I could, Emilio thinks). You, the soldier says to a middle-aged dark-skinned man a few rows ahead of them, show me your papers. The man pulls out his ID and the soldier takes it, looks at it and then at the man, back at the photograph, and then returns it. He asks a young girl for hers and after handing it back, turns and exits. The bus begins moving once more and Emilio relaxes a little bit into his seat and takes a quick look at Matilde and can see she has removed her hand from Juan's grasp. The movie has resumed playing and the comedian is making strange facial gestures and everyone laughs.

They drive another hour and a half and he dozes until the bus is stopped again and another soldier boards. Emilio feels the familiar tightening inside his body when he sees the army uniform, the black boots. He keeps his eyes down, his right hand in his pocket.

Everybody off, the soldier says.

The passengers disembark and Emilio makes his way to a shaded area beneath a metal awning. The soldier has boarded the bus with a large darkgrey dog and Emilio can see the animal sniffing the seats and floor while the soldier guides it down the center aisle.

A different soldier asks the driver to open the luggage compartments and the soldier with the dog comes outside and inspects the cargo areas beneath the bus.

Two soldiers with black rifles strapped to their chests look closely at the circle of passengers waiting beneath the awning in the shade. The passengers are mostly quiet except for a few teenagers chatting in lively voices and texting on their mobile phones. Emilio notices Juan is holding Matilde's hand again, he looks away toward an elderly couple to his right. He tries to appear calm and unconcerned.

Okay, a soldier says, you can go.

Night is descending. Another movie plays, a romance. The bus moves north across the changing landscape and the next movie is a loud police thriller. Emilio tries to sleep but cannot and watches the movie with the other travelers like him who cannot find repose. They should be in El Sásabe within the hour.

Three hours later he and Matilde walk into a hotel room. They ate in the restaurant next door and he ordered beef and rice and beans and she wasn't very hungry but had eaten a small bowl of soup. They can still feel the heat of the day even though the sun descended hours ago. El Sásabe is hot and dry.

She turns on the television and sits on the bed and tells him she is so happy they were able to pay for a room with air conditioning. It's still so warm outside, she says, is this how the weather will be in Arizona?

I think so, he says, and lies next to her on the bed with the air conditioning unit blasting and the sounds of a TV show filling up the room.

We have at least one more day before Pedro and William get here, he says, we can relax.

Oh good, she says, and she changes the channels in search of a movie or sitcom that interests her.

He closes his eyes. Her leg touches his leg hip to ankle, and he wishes he didn't feel so on edge.

It was so comfortable on the autobus, no?

Yes, he says from behind his closed eyes, and he hears the changing volume and voices of game shows and talk shows and commercials as she continues running through the channels and he realizes he also hears English.

Look, she says, it's an American one.

He opens his eyes to see the faces of two fair-haired blue-eyed actors with bright smiling faces and mannequin movements in the front seat of a car. Then a shot of the happy family as they drive along a tree-lined street of large neocolonial houses and manicured green lawns, white rose bushes, geometric hedges. It is all familiar: the actors' speech and gestures, the moving images of American suburbs, the well-dressed and decorous white parents and their polite, handsome children in the backseat. And it is an illusion: an advertisement for the latest model of a luxury four-door sedan. We are close to the border so we must be getting some American channels, he says.

She doesn't find anything she likes and she turns off the television. He has closed his eyes again. There is only the hum of the air conditioning unit inside the room now, one dim overhead light, and his unabated desire inside him. I want to kiss her, he thinks, if only I could kiss her.

Imagine the lucky ones, she says, who get on a first class bus whenever they wish and travel anywhere they would like to go.

Yes, he says.

The fortunate ones born into a rich country. We who were born into the poor nations are luckless.

Yes, he says, without really having heard what she said. He concentrates on trying to relax, perhaps fall asleep.

It's been a month.

The steep descent in the pitch of her voice at the word *month* upsets his concentration and he opens his eyes. He turns his head toward her. He can see the sadness. We have to put forth our best effort, Matilde, he says. You must not lose faith.

She turns to face him. You're not a believer, she says.

I believe in you. He smiles at her.

Ay, Emilio, you're so crazy sometimes. She smiles back at him and then leans over and kisses him on the mouth.

The kiss lights him on fire. He sits up and looks into her dark eyes and she looks at him openly. They kiss again, at first tentatively, slowly, and then with increasing passion. He touches his tongue against her lips, then her tongue, and he says I want to touch you everywhere.

Okay, she says.

They resume kissing for a time and then he says, I want to see you, feel your skin against mine, and she says okay. Yes. He removes her shirt and her bra and finally he sees the beautiful body of which he has dreamed and the perfect small breasts and he takes off his own shirt and kisses the skin above her collarbones, at her heart, moves from one breast and then to the other. He hears the pleasure in her voice when she says his name tenderly. He presses his chest against hers and holds her gently and then tightly. She caresses his back, head, and arms. She says his name again, using the diminutive for the first time since they met.

He returns to her lips and kisses the new brackets that hold them and then her eyes and nose and chin, the point at the middle of her brow above the bridge of her nose, and then her mouth again, he sucks her tongue gently.

He rubs her stomach, he caresses her ribs. He cups his hand over her pubis over the fabric of her blue jeans.

I don't know if it will be okay, she whispers, and the strain has returned in her voice: anxiety filling it up like water does a glass.

He moves the palm of his hand to her breastbone and the skin over her heart and he presses gently but firmly against it to get her attention. He looks into the brown and black of her eyes and tells her that he has never before felt for anyone what he does for her.

How can you be sure?

I knew from the outset. From the riverbank. When I saw you standing there alone in that red tee shirt.

They sit up. He touches her breasts, her brown nipples. He licks them.

She moans softly.

Let me see you, she says.

He stands and removes his jeans and his underwear and she watches him. His cock is erect and he says that he loves her when he turns to face her.

I can see that, she says, and they both laugh and the tension lessens for a moment.

They pull the covers back on the bed and he takes off the rest of her clothes and they lie facing each other now on their sides, skin to skin from their feet to their chests. They breathe in each other's breaths for several moments. He marvels again at her beauty, her breasts with their large brown nipples, her lean legs and the black apex of her sex, at how much he wants to fold himself inside of her, pleasure her, and obliterate himself inside her body.

He rubs his hands up and down her legs, around to her ass. He moves down the bed and opens her legs and looks at her black and red labia, he smells her secretions and touches the skin with his fingers and coats his fingers with her fluids. He then touches her with his lips and tongue and she jumps slightly and he puts one finger and then another inside her. He hears the desire in her voice. Her moans. I love your smell, he tells her, I have loved it all these weeks.

She blushes and laughs and says, what?

It's you, he says.

She smiles and takes hold of his cock with her hand and guides him to the entrance of her vagina; she places her hands on his shoulders and pulls him toward her.

Okay? he asks.

Okay, she answers, and he puts his cock inside her body. And when she looks at him darkly, and he looks deep into her eyes, he thinks for a moment that he can see himself, as if he were Matilde now looking out from her eyes, and then he can't see any longer for he is unstoppably moving and beyond vision and thinking to only feels, and then beyond that also.

He can hear her breath slowing, he can hear the air conditioner humming loudly. His breath is also returning to normal, but now there is a new disturbance inside him. Something he has never known before. Without the overwhelming desire of the last several days, the other thing only rushes inside him more explicitly, fills out, expands: how he wants to care for her, the love he feels for her. And then a small amount of guilt overtakes him because in the past there had always been a diminution of his feelings after sex (even if only momentarily), as it had been with Antonia (although he never admitted it to her, or to himself) but perhaps he hadn't even realized it, for he had had nothing to compare it to, and that too is different with Matilde.

I feel good everywhere, she says.

I feel good everywhere too, he says.

But I am sleepy now. She turns from him onto her side. We should rest. Sweet dreams, Milo.

He rolls over and presses his belly to her back and he puts his arm around her. He wonders if he will have strange vivid dreams tonight, as he has most nights since leaving Todos Santos. Then he realizes that for whatever reason he can no longer recall them since Mexico City.

Sweet dreams, Mati.

In the morning he reaches for her and she for him and they continue to discover the topography of each other's bodies. How when he gently bites the side of her neck, or pulls strongly at her nipples, she becomes more aroused; that he loves the palms of her hands pressed against his back, thighs, and holding his ass. They stay in the room until they are ravenous and leave to eat in the same restaurant and then return and bathe and climb back into bed to lie together. It's different making love with you, she says, because you want to please me so much. A blush rises up her throat and onto her cheeks.

I want to make you come again and again, he says, I want to make you happy.

The two new lovers feel a burgeoning joy inside of the day. All of its hours belong to them, and they find something venerable and tender along its progression.

Late in the evening, the telephone starts to ring and the heavy thing in Emilio's chest rereturns and tightens because he is not sure who could be calling them. He looks at Matilde and the mask of fear is back on her face. After more than a dozen rings he picks up the receiver.

Hello?

I've got thirty little chickens packed up and ready to go.

What, he says, what? Who is calling?

The line goes dead. Then he realizes the caller must have been trying to reach a smuggler leaving tonight and had dialed their room number incorrectly.

There is a knock on the door of their room at four in the afternoon the next day. They gaze at each other for a quick moment:

they made love all morning but have been dressed since noon and waiting and their time alone has ended. Pedro's voice through the door announces, We're here, muchachos!

Matilde embraces Pedro asking anxiously if everything is okay. Are you well?

Yes, Pedro says, we're just hungry and a little tired and we need a shower.

William looks exhausted and doesn't say anything except that he wants a cold drink. Pedro has large dark circles underneath his eyes. Emilio tells them the shower has ample hot water and afterward we'll go eat something.

You look content, Pedro says to Matilde when he emerges from the bathroom half an hour later and sees her sitting next to Emilio on one of the two beds.

We've had ample time to rest, Emilio says.

Matilde doesn't say anything but a red curtain rises from her chest to her cheeks.

They go to a small restaurant down the street for dinner and Pedro has his first beer since he set out from Tegucigalpa.

My God, Pedro says as he lifts the brown glass bottle into the air, it was worth the wait and all the effort!

The four sit at a round table and listen to the norteña music playing loudly on the speakers and drink their beers while they wait for their food.

Perhaps He should have advocated beer and not only wine for His children? Pedro jokes and asks the waitress for another.

Their entrées arrive and they eat and listen to the music while the hot night air swirls in the moving fan above their heads.

For the moment, I feel almost normal: a regular customer eating a regular meal in a restaurant with his friends, Emilio thinks.

It is a basic pleasure: dinner, music, a cold beer, and she is at my side. He looks at her for a moment and she meets his gaze and then looks down. Pedro has a third Pacífico and then they return to the room and he and William fall asleep within minutes.

Emilio can feel the electricity between them again stronger than ever as they lie in bed. He quietly makes her orgasm with his fingers and she returns the pleasure with her hand. They smile into the darkness and he whispers how he loves her. She says that she didn't expect it, but she feels it too. They sleep facing each other, his arm on her waist and hand at her back.

Early the next morning, he and Pedro and William go to pick up the wires each is receiving from family members in the US to pay their guide and to buy the things Chaco told them they will need for the trek: gallon jugs of water; a change of clothes (American-looking, he'd said); an extra pair of shoes; enough food for two days (he said they would have to walk just a few hours before getting picked up by the van on the other side, but as a precaution); deodorant (to smell good when you arrive); a hat (if you want).

We will meet you in front of the pharmacy at three-thirty, Chaco said.

By 9:00 AM it is already hot outside. William and Pedro say they feel rested, but Emilio can see in their faces that they are tired. Pedro still has dark-black circles underneath his eyes, and his cough has returned.

Are you sure you don't want to rest for another day or two? Emilio asks on their way to the market.

Chaco said he wasn't taking another group across for another ten days, Pedro says. I'll be okay, muchacho. We are close now. We'll have all the time in the world to rest when we get to Arizona.

They return to the room after they have made their purchases and prepare to check out. Matilde leaves the makeup he bought her in Mexico City in the room. I'll buy you more when we get across the line, Emilio says when she looks disappointed to leave some of her new things. I'm leaving my journal and pen, I didn't even use them, and an extra shirt. Chaco said don't carry more than necessary.

They each have a backpack with their provisions. Emilio carries a button-down shirt, a change of underwear, socks, shoes, jeans. He carries his new toothbrush and a can of antiperspirant. He has corn tortillas, two tins of sardines, one of beans, some chiles, a piece of white cheese, and a flashlight. He tucked one hundred dollars cash into the waistband of his pants. And he can't help but think again of what he does not carry because he lost it along the way: his silver watch, his Nikes, his red cap and nylon jacket, the green backpack he used in school for so many years. Countless items crisscross the earth's surface, he thinks, with more ease than ever in human history, including all of the things I am carrying today that were manufactured in China and purchased in northern Mexico and sit inside a blue bag on the back of a man who is only trying to get back home. And the winch behind his chest turns and pulls its familiar steel cord from his bowels toward his stomach and he puts his hand into the new jeans pocket and fingers the white stone and it is the one object he has been able to keep with him for five thousand miles: from its origin at Muir Beach, California, to Todos Santos Cuchumatán, Guatemala, through Mexico, and now finally across the Sonoran Desert.

Outside it is hot and dry and the temperature is already one hundred degrees. The sunshine climbs brightly over every surface.

He begins to sweat as soon as they exit the hotel building.

It's so hot already, Matilde says.

They have four more hours yet before they need to meet Chaco and they go to a small restaurant and have a meal. Pedro orders a beer with his steak.

So cold and delicious, Pedro says. Maybe I should have one more?

We have to walk now, better to wait until we get to the other side, Matilde says, we'll relax in Phoenix.

Pedro says he didn't drink any beer for a whole month and that he doesn't want to wait, and he orders one more. It won't hurt anything, he says.

They sit in the air conditioned restaurant after they have finished eating and watch the small television hanging in the corner until it is close to three o'clock and Emilio says they should go. Everyone is a little jumpy; it's good to finally get moving.

Two vans await them in front of the pharmacy and a group of fifteen stand nearby. Chaco arrives with two young men and they load ten people into each vehicle, many more than there are seats for. Everyone crams in together tightly. It's a twenty-minute drive, companions, Chaco says, not too far. The vans start up and head in the direction of the desiccated hills behind the town.

Matilde sits on Emilio's lap and Pedro is hunched over near the side door. William sits squeezed in the back with four other men. No one talks very much during the drive, it is the reticence of trepidation and some hopefulness. They are mostly male passengers in the van except for a small child and the child's young mother who sit up front.

The vans finally stop two hours later. As soon as the doors open Pedro runs behind a bush to urinate with several other men.

The migrants now gather around Chaco with the other coyotes: an adolescent who looks no older than William and goes by Rabbit, and a young man with closely shaved dark hair and large dark sunglasses called Nexo. They are twenty in their group of little chickens.

Señores, Chaco says, you'll be across the line soon. But it turns out I have other business I must attend to today in El Sásabe, so Rabbit and Nexo will guide you.

What? an older Oaxacan man says, we hired you, not them.

Señores, I trained them myself, they're the best. Now it's time to get going. Watch your step. If you fall behind they can't wait for you or the migra will get all of you. If you get delayed, wait where you are and after the migra picks you up and dumps you back at the border I'll meet you in El Sásabe for another try. Ladies, there are rattlesnakes and scorpions, so be careful when you need to relieve yourselves in the desert.

The group begins walking. They are sixteen men, three women, and one child. Oaxacans, Guatemalans, Veracruzanos, Hondurans, and two men in their twenties from Mexico City. They are mostly people from the green lush lands of the south. They don't know the desert or the dry heat or its force. They are silent. They feel anxious because the plans have changed, but they all follow the instructions and follow Nexo. The dirt trail before them is filled with trash. As they walk they see discarded water bottles, old clothes, empty food wrappers, a hair brush. It is six o'clock, it is still hot, and the light is bright and they are all sweating but they hope the heat is waning. The low dry hills rise above them. The white rippling clouds sit low in the light-blue sky and big thorny cacti and brittle bush and ocotillo lie at intervals. Sand and rocks beneath their feet. Creosote and a palo verde tree.

Pedro is in line behind the older Oaxacan man, followed by

Matilde, then Emilio, and William behind him. She carries her black backpack and a one-gallon jug of water in her hand. Emilio is holding a jug of water in each hand and his backpack makes him even hotter; the back of his tee shirt is already soaked through with his sweat and he is excited that in only a more few hours he will be back in the United States. Finally, he thinks, I'll be on American soil.

The sun is setting; the air and the ground remain hot. This is the strongest heat any of the walkers has ever known. They are thirsty. Their mouths begin to dry. Just a little bit of water, they think, and they take a sip of their water and their throats dry out between each small sip. Their lips soon begin to crack and they are licking their lips to soothe them and they sweat and the water of their bodies wets their clothes and the heat dries it. They hear the howls of animals and the stars begin to shine in the sky overhead and each tries to avoid twisting his ankle and keep up with the group and walks. They are more thirsty. If they are not drinking, the roofs of their mouths and tongues become sticky and they desire water and their spit starts to turn to paste in their mouths. They lick their lips continuously. They cross a barbed wire fence and now they are in the United States. We have made it across the line, Emilio thinks, and it's so hot and I'm thirsty, I have a bad taste in my mouth—he takes another sip of his water—and after all the travels, the travails, it was nothing more than a broken-down fence between the two nations, no more than flimsy wires keeping me out. And the vast desert. Only a few more hours to go now. One more day until I am back.

The walkers go as quietly as they can. Each man and each woman keeps his and her own thoughts. The ground does not cool and for the old Oaxacan who walks in plastic sandals, his feet have been burning him a long time. Matilde's legs ache and her fingers hurt from holding the gallon of water which, walking and drinking, begins to lose its weight. They think about the step in front of them and the next one. Emilio's hot feet sweat inside of his tennis shoes and swell in the night.

They walk for hours. They drink the precious water from their jugs and think soon we'll be in Phoenix. Just one more sip of water. It's so dry. Just one small sip. Phoenix must be close, just over this next rise.

They are walking and drinking and their throats are dry and their tongues are sticky and the heat is caustic and like a demon it sucks, bit by bit, the moisture from their bodies.

Just one more sip.

We'll be there soon.

It's been so many hours already, another small sip can't hurt.

At midnight, the thin sliver of the waning crescent moon rises above their heads. The hot air continues to dry their throats and mouths. Emilio is licking his lips and Matilde licks and presses her lips together, and all of their lips swell and crack further. The heat is endless in the darkness and they walk in it and each step is the step before the next one. Only America lies ahead of them, only the promised land they were dreaming of in Guatemala and Honduras and Oaxaca and Veracruz and the capital.

Each migrant does his best to follow the person in front of him. Nexo and Rabbit lead the way.

No noise, señores, or flashlights, Nexo said, or the migra will find us. We'll be there soon.

Matilde is saying to herself please God help me God, give me the strength, Señor, for this last leg of our journey. She is thinking about Katerin and Jorge Luis and if they are sleeping peacefully and how when she kissed them goodbye before she left they didn't cry because they were too young to know what the goodbying meant. And of their small bodies, sweet smells, and their "I love you Mami," and please dear Lord help me for my children to make it across the desert tonight so that we will be in the place of my dream and everything will be better, my little children will be safer, secure and content after I cross this desert tonight and get out of this heat. And for the one I've known three weeks who walks behind me.

Large blisters reform on Emilio's feet and on hers. His feet are burning, hers have also swelled in her shoes. The rocks and the dirt and sand are hot and abrasive and their ankles turning and leg muscles cramping and invisible thorns tear at their clothes from every bush and tree and tall cactus, and they can hear in the darkness how some of the others are crying out, their suffering, and the child is crying and the mother tries to quiet her. Some walk with twisted ankles now and they are moaning, walking; the old man from Oaxaca limps in front of Pedro whispering, I turned my ankle and it hurts; when will we get there, Señor Nexo, when will we arrive?

Grey light and the lightening at the horizon, the lifting of darkness at dawn. The pink luminescence is upon the distant mountains and as the yellow orb rises into view, the heat augments and the sun begins to burn upon them. The Sonoran Desert is no place for walkers. They have been hiking for fourteen hours already. The light commences to beat sharply against their faces and eyes and exposed arms. Why didn't I bring a hat, Emilio thinks, how could I have been so stupid as to not purchase a new one? The sun pierces his eyes and he, like the others, keeps his head tilted to the ground to protect them from the glare.

Two hours pass and they are walking, stumbling, and the sun is burning hotter and starker upon them.

Okay, señores, we'll rest here during the hottest part of the day. We're almost there. Don't worry, Nexo says.

You said we were almost there at sunrise, one of the men from Mexico City says, that we were close to the pick-up spot where the air conditioned vans would meet us to drive us to the safe house. Do you know where we are?

It's okay, Nexo says, his eyes remain hidden behind his dark lenses, don't worry, we're close. We'll just rest for a few hours during the hottest part of the day. He and Rabbit go off from the group to find some shade.

The group huddles together beneath the thorny mesquite trees and the creosote in the narrow shade and they hope they will not find rattlesnakes sleeping there. They see garbage spread out across the rest area: discarded plastic bags of food, tin cans, old clothes, and empty water containers; they are not the first to stop here. Human feces can be seen in small piles off the foot paths.

The ground is hot, and the desert flora offers little protection from the bright yellow light.

Emilio sits with Matilde, Pedro, and William, each on his backpack, after they have pulled out some of their food. The cheese has melted and is ruined and Emilio opens a tin of sardines and everything is hot and nearly impossible to consume. Matilde says she is not hungry. He sees that her eyes are sinking into her skull and how her face is covered in white salt patches from sweat and red scratches from thorns; her pallor is ashen.

You must eat, he says, to maintain your strength.

She forces herself to eat a tortilla. It is mid-morning and they are all exhausted and they are almost out of water. The water which remains inside the plastic jugs is as hot as coffee and burns their mouths when they take a sip. The temperature continues to rise; it is well over one hundred and ten degrees now.

To be honest, muchachitos, Pedro says, I don't feel too good.

He is coughing again.

I'm a little dizzy. A little nauseated. My legs hurt, my feet are fat and pain me in these shoes.

Lie down, Matilde says, you'll feel better. You just need to rest. We haven't slept.

She makes him drink a few sips of water and eat a few bites of tortilla and he closes his eyes. His face is also covered in white patches and he looks pale.

How much longer? one of the Veracruzanos yells out to Nexo and Rabbit, but the coyotes don't reply.

The group of twenty are mostly quiet and everyone is thirsty and thinking of cold water and hoping the air conditioned van is waiting for them over the next rise. Only a little bit farther, each says to himself, and we'll be there, we'll rest easy when we arrive. The child is sleeping in her mother's arms, her face salt-streaked and burned. A kind Veracruzano carried her most of the night when the girl's mother could not support her weight any longer.

The land—dry, wild, and barren—stretches out from them and it feels to Emilio as if they are on another planet, hundreds of miles from anything I have ever known but it could be thousands because I have never before known this kind of heat and sun and dryness. He is thinking about cold water and cold soda and cold beer and an enormous cold mountain lake which he could bathe in and drink from. His feet and legs are swollen like hers, like Pedro's and William's. Pedro's eyes remain closed and his eyes are sunken into his face and his lips terribly cracked; there are numerous wounds on his arms where thorns cut and pierced the skin.

My feet burn, Matilde says to Emilio.

Mine too. Have another small sip of water.

I think Pedro has already finished his, she says.

They hear a helicopter in the distance.

Everyone down and don't move! Nexo yells.

They scramble closer to the thorny bushes. Emilio stabs his hand on one of the long thorns and the wound bleeds slowly. The helicopter doesn't come nearer and instead veers east.

God have mercy on us, the lady with the child says. She is out of water and begs the man who carried her child for some of his. He shares it with her.

The day heats up, the ground heats up further.

Are we close? they are asking. Nexo and Rabbit are silent. They still appear to be napping.

Do you know where we are?

Will we get to the air conditioned vans soon?

By dinner?

The child is crying and the old Oaxacan man says, I don't think I can walk any farther. I've twisted my ankle and I think it's broken, look how swollen it is becoming, and my tongue is swollen and I don't have any more water. Water, please, someone.

One of the young Oaxacans shares some of his.

The sun overhead is upon everything and cutting into their eyes and mouths and noses and throats and lungs and pulling along with the air every bit of moisture from their bodies. There is little sweat left in them. They are only dry and drying.

The sun is our enemy, Emilio thinks. The sun could be God.

He tries to sleep.

In the late afternoon when the sun has moved farther westward in the sky and the heat has not abated, the air still attacking all of them, Rabbit stands up and says they need to get moving. It's time to go, we're close.

The group stands on its tired and swollen legs, scratched and sunburned, every muscle is sore and their feet are covered with open sores inside their shoes. They are all thirsty; they are all unbearably hot.

The old man tries to stand but his ankle is too large to walk on now. Another Oaxacan gives him his half-full jug of water and they leave the old man behind beneath a palo verde tree.

The migra will pick you up soon, Nexo says to him.

They all feel badly and the man says, Please tell my children I'll make it next time.

They leave him in the barren desert beneath the barren tree and hope the migra will find him quickly. Only God and not even the lizards can live here.

They walk.

The light is bright white-yellow on everything, on their bodies and stabbing their eyes. Emilio's upper eyelids hold closely to his bottom lids; he is squinting fiercely. Why didn't I buy a new baseball cap in El Sásabe, he laments again, I was so stupid. The sun beats strongly against his black hair and scalp; if only they hadn't taken my red cap from me in Tapachula.

There are large rocks and burning sand and his feet burn and his nose and lips and cheeks and arms and scalp and his eyelids: all burning, all hotter. My lungs can't hold this air, he thinks, they'll singe, incinerate, and when the heat kills then the sun could be a murderer because my brain is floating in liquid and the sun is murdering water so it is murdering the cushion of liquid around my brain and killing me and the girl I love.

She is walking behind William and Emilio walks behind her. Pedro now walks behind him. They are gaining elevation and the group is quiet and the child cries at times and then she is silent and the same kind Veracruzano carries her and the mother walks behind him; she is limping and her left ankle is enormous around the edges of her black shoe from when she twisted it over an hour ago.

Emilio's nose starts to bleed and the red blood rushes down his face. Can we stop, I want to stop, he thinks as he walks. He is thinking of water and of ice in water and of the saltwater bay near his home and a swimming pool to crawl into and a mountain lake to bathe in and drink from. The sun is a killer and appalling and he pushes his thick tongue over his cracked lips and he tastes his own blood. His throat is a dry cavity and like the sand he walks across, gritty and painful, and his saliva is viscous and he has a terrible metallic taste in his mouth. He lifts his feet and he wants to kill the rocks and the sun and cacti and the sharpness of the light of the thorns of the stones which are murdering them. Blood on his chin throat and shirt.

He is thinking of the mountain lake. He sees it in the distance. Is that it? He walks and follows.

The sun finally sets and night rises and the hours pass and the child cries again and some of the group is falling behind and he doesn't know if they are the Oaxacans or the Veracruzanos because his vision is limited, but perhaps that is the road ahead, perhaps those are city lights? Matilde, he says from time to time into the silence of the walkers, Matilde, you're okay, keep moving, and thinks: it is killing, the hot earth and the hot air killing everything, killing us; but to her only says, everything is okay, keep going, we'll make it, it's all right. She is crying and she is saying my feet are on fire, Emilio, and my face is burnt down to the bones and my scalp and my eyes hurt. And he says, we'll make it, it's okay we've come so far (and: kill kill kill in himself to himself) and his back hurts, his legs are stones, the soles of his feet are blistered and bleeding, and where the thorns pierced his hands and arms there are small red wounds. His saliva is sand in his metal mouth. His throat begs him for a little water: please, please give me some; it closes in on him, strangles him. His jug is almost empty now, just one more little hot sip for my metal mouth and throat, he thinks, and then he drops the jug in the desert landscape like the other one he left miles and miles ago.

The sun is gone from the sky but its force is still upon them, beneath them: the sand cooks anything it touches and our bodies, he thinks, cooks it like a piece of beef or chicken, and that is why they call us the little chickens because they are going to eat us up in the desert, and who are Nexo and Rabbit, and maybe they want to kill kill kill like the yellow star and the Sonoran. Maybe we are lost after all?

He hears Pedro stumble behind him and call out.

I can't walk farther, Pedro says. I can't walk anymore, muchachos. I give up. God, I give up. I can't. No more. It's enough.

Emilio turns back to him and says, just a few more steps. You can do it, you must give it your best. William, do you still have some?

William says that he has a quarter remaining in his jug.

Give him a few sips, we're close now.

I'm tired, Pedro says, I'm very tired. Can you see my swollen ankles? Do you think my wife is home from work?

You must keep walking, Pedro, Emilio says, we can't stop, we'll lose the group. Have courage.

And Pedro is limping along and speaking to his wife and children and talking about water and cool air and the green land of his birth and of life.

Can you give him a little more? Emilio asks.

William makes Pedro take another sip and they are trying not to lose the group and the desert air is taking everything from them: their bodies' last vestiges of moisture deep inside their organs and from the blood and moving over and high into my brain, Emilio thinks, to murder, to kill. Everything is going, he thinks; the winch and wire now molten inside him.

The twenty-one walking, twenty-one mouths dried up, and the forty-two feet expanded in their shoes and everyone's skin covered in sores. Their legs are fatter and they still sweat, but they can't tell any longer if they are sweating because the moisture evaporates so quickly. They go up an incline and down and over a plain and forward through creosote and prickly pear and they twist blindly around the rocks hoping they won't step on the coiled snakes or into the scorpion's sting; each focuses on the man or woman in front of him.

The sun rises and they have not stopped all night. Thirteen hours have passed since they began walking again.

One man who is out of water urinates into his plastic container to save his piss: it is a dark yellow liquid. He is not the only one.

We can't drink it once it turns brown, one of the Veracruzanos says.

We should have saved ours from earlier, his brother says.

Exhaustion in the sunken eyes and burnt skin and the viscous eyeballs begin to dry out, the blood vessels to burst. They feel feverish and then some of them oddly begin to feel cold; the child does not cry any longer, she only sleeps now. The twenty-one throats and mouths and tongues can't find moisture upon anything. Their throats click when they speak.

The temperature continues to rise.

Okay, Nexo says, we'll find a place to rest.

You promised me and my brother we'd make it in one day, the Veracruzano says. We've been walking for two. We must have walked eighty kilometers already. We are tired.

We'll be there soon. Don't worry, it was to avoid the migra. Did you want to get caught?

Many of us are out of water, one of the young Oaxacan farmers says.

Chht. Quiet. We'll be there soon. You'll have lots of water soon. Don't worry. There's a road one kilometer from here. We're very close now.

They try to find some silver shade, but here there is less of it and the sun is making yellow helmets upon their heads and baking their skins browner to black and their insides; the temperature of their blood and viscera rising.

Emilio is thinking about water. He is thinking about a mountain lake that he could bathe in and drink from. Cool liquid on my body, in my body. Water is our savior.

And Pedro is saying, see what my wife has prepared! How happy she looks when the children have returned home from school!

William has a small amount of water remaining in his jug, hot almost to boiling. Matilde makes Pedro drink it.

It burns, Pedro says. It burns me, Señor.

They hear another helicopter in the distance.

Mosquitoes, Nexo says, hide!

They try to conceal themselves behind the small bushes and their clothes are torn by the mesquite and cacti, but they are tired and moving slowly and the helicopter spots their group. The machine comes closer and the pilot lowers it nearer to the ground as if to press its blades down on them. The rapidly moving machine and loud noise frighten everyone and make a hot dusty whirlwind. The migrants run out of their hiding places, terrified, into the open white-hot day, and scatter. Emilio runs with Matilde, and she pulls Pedro along behind her. The three of them climb a rocky incline and hide behind large burning boulders inside their thin pockets of shade. Within minutes, Border Patrol arrives on the creosote plain and the helicopter lifts up and departs. Emilio can hear the trucks' engines from where they crouch. The guards get out and scream obscenities in English and heavily accented Spanish. They pull out their guns and threaten everyone and within little time handcuff and load sixteen migrants and the two coyotes into their vehicles. William climbs into a truck with the Oaxacans.

The vehicles depart and the desert returns to stillness and quiet.

I don't want to walk any farther, Pedro says. My wife is so beautiful. Ana, I love you.

Everything is okay, Pedro, Matilde tells him. Ana is in Honduras, but we are close, we'll be in Phoenix soon. The guide said it's only one kilometer to the road in that direction. We have to keep going, we are almost there.

The three of them begin to walk again. They are out of water and the day is hotter, brighter; it crashes upon them. They walk in the direction Nexo had indicated. Pedro is stumbling along and falling behind, a dark figure against the rising swirls of air and light.

Do you think the road is really this way? Matilde asks.

We must go a little farther, Emilio says.

They wait for Pedro.

Ana, Pedro says, and he lifts his wan face, let's go inside.

Pedro, Matilde says, we are in the desert, we are in the North. It's hot, but we'll be okay. Just a little bit farther. We are walking to the road. You'll see her again. But first we must get to the road, to Phoenix.

Blood is dried all around Pedro's nose and his face is terribly burned. His eyes are sunken and his skin has begun to look like leather. He is saying, because I am in my rightful place. He stumbles along and talks with his wife and falls onto the dirt, and it burns his skin further and they realize he has fallen and turn back to help him.

Pedro, get up, Matilde says. You must give it your best effort now. God is with you, He is with us. Just a little bit more to the road and we'll get water. Get up, your family needs you, there's a fourth one on the way, remember?

And Emilio is thinking how the killer is killing and the sun is God and the sun is the murderer and this earth that wants to cook him and her and his flesh is meat and cattle and dogs and fish and chicken are for eating and he ate them like a god and now the jackals and the vultures will consume him at their own barbeque. And why not a large mountain lake he could bathe in and cool himself by and drink from also?

Oh God, Emilio says, and he puts his knees into the burning dirt at Pedro's side. Matilde asks him if he can pull Pedro up and put him onto his back and he says that he can. She tells him they must hurry and get to the road and find the migra or Pedro could die and they could all die out here. (I don't want to die I only want water and why is the sun a killer and all of the hot burning on me and the earth?)

I can do it, he says, and he removes his backpack and then slowly lifts Pedro onto his back.

Can you see my sweet girls and the boy? Pedro whispers into his neck. I am in my rightful place and everything is good again.

Yes, Emilio says, and he staggers along the wide, brown barren landscape beneath the heavy body of his friend and his guide, and sand and creosote and cactus cut him and small sharp stones. Pedro has fallen silent and the heat is killing and the air has taken everything from their skin. Matilde walks at his side. She is talking, saying, I think I see the road, it's there, the road is just a bit farther. And the road is not there and the pilgrims wander alone in the wilderness.

Emilio takes a step and thinks, one more step, takes it and pauses and then takes one more. He slowly moves across the landscape with his burden and she is saying, just a bit farther, Emilio, I think I see the road.

The sun is at its zenith and Pedro's tongue is pushing out of his mouth and purpling now, his eyes moving even deeper into their sockets as they shrivel and redden.

Pedro's weight is heavier and heavier on him and his own head is becoming an iron helmet now. Emilio is thinking of his mother and of putting one foot in front of the other and thinking one step one more step and: Mother you have always been at the earth's center and: Mother why did God put us here in this desert to die for meat?

Matilde is beside him. She is telling him, Emilio, God is with us, Emilio, you must keep going. Just a little farther. Keep walking, Emilio. Have faith. Have courage. I think I see the road.

Pedro's body is His burden on his back and the sun is his enemy and he is dizzy and nauseated and he falls, finally, to the ground. The dirt, sand, and stones singe his knees, his chest, and face and Pedro lies on top of him, and Emilio says I can't walk anymore, Matilde, I'm too tired.

Pedro falls off of his back onto the killer earth, shriveling and cooking, and he does not open his eyes.

The earth burns everything it touches.

Then Pedro opens them. Mother, he says, Anita, and he looks straight up into the infernal star that is both giver of life and of death. I will look, he says, I will see it as it comes for me. He is frothing at the mouth now, yellow and bilious.

Get up, Matilde is screaming at them. Just a few more steps, get up, we have to move forward or we'll die. I'll not perish in this godforsaken desert because I have my children and you have your families, now stand up, Emilio, please, you can, and you will. We'll carry him together. Get up, I said, and she screams it at him: get up getup. And the scream is only a rasp out of her dry, clicking throat, but Emilio feels her anger, her urgency, her sheer strength of will moves him from his chest to his hands and knees on the broiling desert floor and the sun beats the back of his iron head, his body, but she is stronger than the sun, Emilio thinks, and he stands.

He is in the kitchen and his mother is offering him a glass of water. He is reaching out his arm to take it and the killer is back, killing his brain and his organs, and nausea rises up strongly to annihilate the day and he vomits onto the sand.

Emilio, she yells at him, grabs his arms.

He looks at her and wipes his mouth with his shirt and then bends down and grabs Pedro from beneath the shoulders. She holds his legs and from somewhere deep inside her her faith is lifting Pedro and telling Emilio to lift him up and she is praying dear God please, please give me the strength; I have always believed in You, I have always been Your servant. And she is telling Emilio to walk and he is following her commands and listening to his mother and trying to reach the glass she has extended toward him and Antonia runs away from him and this girl won't stop, doesn't leave, endures; her: move it, keep going, one more step, I think I see the road. They walk over a small rise on the rocks and thorns and oven of this white earth, it claws at their feet and legs, and she is still seeing but his eyes no longer focus and he sees his mother and sisters and finally his father who raises his hand to him from the other side and blesses him. Then a mountain lake, a tall glass of water, but not ten feet in front of them the large blue plastic cylinder shining brightly underneath a palo verde tree.

Emilio, he hears his father say, my son, hold on. The dirt and rocks rise to meet his body again. His mother holds the glass to his mouth, and he drinks from it deeply.

Matilde tells Emilio to put Pedro down and he has collapsed with him onto the burning desert floor. She reads a sign written in Spanish and English and she knows they are saved from this moment. She fills an empty bottle from her backpack at the blue tank and when she takes a sip the hot liquid tastes like plastic and chlorine, but she forces herself to drink it and she hurries back to the two men. They have both shut their eyes and she yells at Emilio to open them and at Pedro, I've found water! She screams again, and her scream is quiet and parched and her throat still clicks. She pours some water onto Pedro's lips and she wets his shirt and she pours more into his mouth. She puts the bottle to Emilio's lips and he opens his eyes and says Dad? in English. She is pouring the hot water in him, on him, telling him to drink it. Open your mouth, she says.

It's too hot, he says, I don't want it.

Open it, she tells him again, and he obeys. He gags but he drinks, and when she turns to give more to Pedro she sees he has opened his eyes and he is looking directly above, past the branches of the palo verde tree, and into the sky. His purple tongue is hanging past his teeth and his brown eyes are red and cooked and she sees how her dear friend, husband to her stepsister Ana, companion on this long journey, and their stalwart leader, and how he has died.

Oh God, oh God, she wails, and she sits down next to him. Her legs are burning and her eyes and Oh dear God, dear Pedro. She begins to sob and she is saying his name and crying, and no tears run out of her tear ducts as the sadness falls heavily down the channel of her throat. Emilio, she says. She goes back to him and puts a little more water into his mouth and she pours it onto his face and washes the rest of the blood and vomit from his lips. Wake up, Emilio. Don't leave me here by myself, Milo, please, Milito, I need you. I love you.

He opens his eyes and Mamá, he says, I was so hot but now I am cold.

She gives him more water and he gags and she makes him drink more and when she begins to feel dizzier, she also drinks.

He looks up at the apparition in front of him and upon her visage he thinks he sees the old chthonic symbol, intersection of heaven and earth, as the hot water moves into his mouth and she gently encourages him and brings him back from the brink.

She refills the bottle again. They have rested and they have drunk their fill.

We must go, she says, we can't spend another night out here. We need to find the road.

They leave Pedro's body behind. They couldn't bury him, but she made a small cross by his head with hot stones and she covers him with his extra clothes and they leave him in the darkest swath of dappled shade they can find next to the blue water tank and the sign:

HUMANE BORDERS FRONTERAS COMPASIVAS
AGUA WATER

Matilde knows Pedro's name and phone number are printed on the inside band of his underwear because they had laughed at him when he insisted on writing it there, and so when his body is found they will be able to identify him and call Ana. Heartbroken now, she walks, and she is saying please God help us, we have to find the road and get help, he's not well either.

Emilio is better since he drank the water, but he remains weak.

He leans on her and they are walking on the hot dirt, their tired and blistered feet always hotter, and sometimes he sees his mother and sometimes he sees his father, and sometimes he strangely begins to feel cold again. His tongue is swollen to the roof of his mouth and pushes outward past his teeth. He sees his sisters and the lake and the glass and then Matilde makes him drink a little bit and he follows her. They move forward and she is his light and guides him.

I see it! she says. The road just ahead.

They stumble forward, making their way toward it, but the farther they walk, the more it moves beyond them. They drink the scalding water until it is gone and the road continues receding and they do not arrive until the sun is beginning to lower in the sky.

Sit here, she says, we must rest. We'll wait until the migra comes.

He is thinking about his swollen tongue and lips and throat and how they collude with the sun to murder, how the air and the dirt are also murdering, cooking him up into barbeque. I only want to find protection from the killer, he thinks, I only hate the sun.

We are going to be okay, she says again. He will not abandon us here. The migra will come soon.

They sit at the side of the two-lane road and she cradles his head in her lap. She is praying and the sunlight is still on them and she shades his burnt face, burnt lips, swollen tongue and eyes with her own body (his face now almost black from its former brown) as well as she can. The migra will be here soon, Milo, Milito my love, hold on.

He sees his mother and she says, My son my son, Milo, why did you run away? I thought that you had died.

And he: Mother Mother, won't you let me inside the house? I only want to come inside once more.

Come in, she says. Come home.

Out of the haze, a dust cloud appears on the road, and then a large blue pickup truck heading toward them. When it gets closer, Matilde can make out a grey-haired man in the front seat and she raises an arm to attract his attention. She waves her hand frantically as he passes by them, but he does not stop his vehicle. She looks down at Emilio and sees his eyes have closed. He looks like he is going. She shifts his hot body deeper into the pocket of her lap and she tries to shield him further. My God, she says, my God. The dust gathers around them and covers them.

She is talking with God. She is saying, we have come so far, dear Lord. She is whispering Emilio's name again and again. She looks up when she hears the noise of the truck's engine as it once again increases: the man has turned around and is returning. The shiny blue vehicle halts not five feet from them and the man opens his door, gets out, and approaches.

Enfermo, he says, in strongly accented Spanish. He points at Emilio.

Matilde starts talking to him rapidly. Por favor, ayúdanos. Necesitamos agua. Por favor, llevamos tres días en el desierto y necesitamos un médico.

The man turns from her and she screams out, por favor, señor, por el amor de Dios, but he continues walking to his truck. She is crying and Emilio opens his eyes. He wants to take off his clothes because they are bothering him and he wants to sleep more than anything and talk with his mother and sisters again and reach for the unattainable glass Mother is holding out to him from the distant mountain lake. And where did Father go. ¿Papá? he says.

The man returns with two bottles of water, opens one and hands it to her.

¡Está fría! she says as she gratefully takes it from his hand and puts the bottle to Emilio's lips, for he has closed his eyes once again.

¡Despiértate! No duermas. Es peligroso dormir. Agua. Toma. Agua fría. Es un milagro. She props him up and begins to pour the cold water into his mouth and the man bends down and stops her with his hand.

Señorita, he says, lento.

The man helps Emilio drink a small amount and then he motions with his hand for Matilde to drink some from the other bottle. Just a little bit of water at a time at first.

After several minutes, Emilio reopens his eyes. The water is cold and it is as if he is drinking it in a dream. He sits up slowly and drinks more. Heaven, he thinks, I am drinking water in heaven. The man poured some on the top of his head and face to cool him and as he drinks more he slowly begins to improve.

¿Dónde encontraste agua fría? he says.

Ya te dije, she says, este señor nos la regaló.

He drinks more of the delicious cold water, thinking it's better than a dream, and his eyes begin to focus again, his head begins to clear. He looks at the man kneeling before him. He sees the heavily wrinkled mottled skin from age and too much sun, small blue eyes, mostly greyed hair. The old man wears old cowboy boots and a baseball cap, a large, round, silver belt buckle presses against his potbelly. Ah no, Emilio thinks, an Arizona redneck.

Most of the water is gone from the bottle and sloshes around in the sack of Emilio's stomach. He looks at her and she looks worried and exhausted. He extends the bottle toward her because he realizes he hasn't shared any of it. She shows him the second bottle she has been drinking from.

¿Es bueno? the man says in his accented stilted Spanish.

I am better, Emilio says to the man in English, thank you so much for the water. It has never tasted so good.

The man appears surprised for a moment when he hears Emilio speak without an accent.

I'm American, Emilio says.

That's good you can speak English, because I only know a few words of Spanish and I had a hard time communicating with her when you were passed out, but my God, son, what were you thinking, crossing the desert in summer? Hundreds die out here every year in this heat.

We were out hiking, he says. We got lost.

You might speak English perfectly, but I can tell you're illegals. Only illegals come through here.

Emilio drinks another sip of the water. The heat is still a killer but diminished for a moment by the cold on him and in him.

I live in Berkeley with my mom and two sisters, he finally says. I know you don't know me, she and I appreciate your kindness, thank you again for stopping. We were out on a hike and became disoriented from the heat.

You looked like you were in bad shape.

Would you be able to give us a lift to a bus stop? I can pay you for the gas. I have some cash on me.

Matilde is watching both of the men, listening to them, unable to comprehend what they are saying.

I'm sorry, son, but I could get into all kinds of trouble for help-ing illegals. Jail time and a half million in fines. I'll alert Border Patrol; you need medical attention and so does your girlfriend. I was going to call them after I saw you, but I decided I'd better stop since you looked like you might be in immediate trouble.

We only need a ride to a bus. We lost our way, that's all, on our hike and the heat got to us. We didn't realize what we were getting ourselves into.

I can leave you some more water and I've got some nuts in the truck, but I'm afraid that's it. It's a felony to aid illegals.

They hear sounds of a helicopter in the distance.

¿Qué está diciendo?, Matilde asks.

I can give you a hundred dollars, Emilio says.

Son, like I said.

Emilio looks the man in the eye and then looks away and he feels a great despair fall upon him. A desperate feeling as large as this awful desert. He turns to Matilde and sees her burnt face and cracked lips and the white salt on her face, the dried blood on her nostrils and all along her arms where the cacti pierced the skin and dozens of sharp thorns cut deeply, and the question in her eyes. He sees how she has suffered and the formidable grace of this girl nonetheless, a girl who walked and rode and deliberately said only forward for the hope she has of bettering her life and her children's lives. She is gaunt and exhausted and her dark-brown eyes are deeper in her skull and she is always, for him, the most beautiful. He looks back at the man again and he decides to take another tack.

Sir, I've never begged in my life, he says to his countryman in their shared language, but I am begging you now. It's true: she and I traveled almost three thousand miles to get here. We have been on the road day and night for weeks. We have not had enough food or water along the way and some terrible things have happened. We lost our friends. I grew up in California, I'm a student at UC Berkeley, and I only want to go home and see my family. And I want to help her. We just need a little assistance, a ride to a bus stop. I'll give you all the money I have on me for your time and the risk. Please.

Son, I tell you, he says, I can't do it. You're not the first I've seen, and I'd get into trouble with the government. You folks just need to stay in your own countries. You'll be all right. Border Patrol will give you something to eat and medical attention before they send you back to Mexico.

Matilde was asking him ¿Nos va a ayudar? Dios nos ayudará, nos ayudó en todo el camino. Ten fé, Emilio.

He listens to her, but in this he has not changed: he is still not a believer. He looks again into the man's face. Do you believe? In God, I mean, he asks him.

I go to church on Sundays. I have my faith, yes.

In all honesty, sir, I don't know what I believe. But I know I might not have made it if you hadn't come along, just as I wouldn't have survived without her.

I don't like to see anyone suffering out here. I'm glad I was able to help you, son. But there are all kinds of checkpoints on these roads and Border Patrol would have found you sooner or later. They'll come and get you. I'll make the call.

The helicopter noise in the distance increases, but the machine has not yet come into view.

Mírale. Es un buen hombre, she says. Se le ve en la cara.

Intenté convencerle llevarnos a una parada de autobús, pero no, Emilio says.

Háblale con tu corazoncito, Milo, como me hablaste a mí.

The grey-haired American stands up.

I'm sorry I can't help you further. I hate to see anyone outside in this heat. It's a killer.

Can I ask your name before you go?

Jonathan Freedman.

Mr. Freedman, I'm Emilio Ramos. I was raised in the church, my mother is a devout woman, and when I was a child she used to read to us from Scripture. I haven't lied to you: I don't know what kind of god I believe in or if I believe. I've felt so hopeless over the last several months. My family is here legally and I've lived here since I was a baby but I'm not allowed to stay, or to return for ten years, if ever. I've seen some bad things as I've tried to get back and I've heard terrible stories about what's happening in Central America and in Mexico. But I have also been the recipient of great kindness and compassion. Since I was a boy my mother would remind me: *Insomuch as you have done it unto the least of these, my brethren, you have done it unto me.* I'm a stranger to you, Mr. Freedman, but I'm begging you to take us to the nearest bus stop in the closest town. We have come so far. We are so close.

John is listening to him and he sees their sun-darkened faces. The dried blood and sweat. The ruined, dusty torn clothes and shoes. The dirty black hair and sunken eyes, chapped faces and lips, the cuts on their arms and hands, the miles they've traveled, their youth, their stink, their fortitude. He is quiet for a moment and sweat drips down the center of his back, along the sides of his face from his scalp, down the insides of his arms. The helicopter noise from ten minutes ago fades into silence as it heads away. He takes a long deep breath and he hears the young man and the young woman doing the same. The desert air hangs between them like a barrier. The day is hot and lonely, the dry mountains and white sky and the earth, long interminable and harsh and wild in the Sonoran.

John squats down again. He leans into Emilio and says put your arms around my neck, son. Can you hold on? Emilio puts his arm around him and John lifts him up and carries him towards his truck. Tell the girl she should follow us.

Ven.

Matilde grabs her backpack.

Can she open the lever?

Ábrelo, Emilio says, and she does it and John lowers Emilio into the truck bed.

I know it's warm in there, but the sun won't be on you and it'll cool off as soon as I blast the AC. It's a twenty-five minute drive to my house where you can get cleaned up. I've got a sports drink in the cab. He goes to the truck cabin and returns and hands Matilde the bottle and tells them to sip from it.

She climbs in next to Emilio.

Keep down, but the windows are tinted, so we should be all right.

John closes the truck bed and goes to the cab and starts it up.

What if he's taking us to the migra? she says.

Listen, Emilio tells her, I just gave this guy a lecture on the Bible. You are the believer among us, you said you could tell he was a good man, so now we have to see it through.

John opens the small window between the cab and the bed of the truck so that they can feel the air-conditioning, which he's put on its highest setting.

They pass two white Border Patrol trucks on South Sasabe Road and John waves to them. He keeps driving till he reaches Highway 86.

John lets them out of the back of the truck after he has pulled through a gate and into the driveway in front of a small ranch house.

No one here but us, John says. My wife passed away four years ago. The boys live in Tucson with their families. Can you walk?

Slowly. My feet are swollen and sore.

I'll help you in, John says, tell the girl to come along.

Vamos adentro.

¿Estás seguro?

Sí.

John helps Emilio to the front door and eases him down onto one of the chairs on the porch and opens the door to the house. It's nothing fancy, he says, but you'll be cool inside.

The house is a simple looking one-story design, old-fashioned, orderly. John helps Emilio to a bedroom and to the large bed.

This was my youngest's room.

I'm sorry I'm so dirty, Emilio says.

Can't be helped.

Matilde follows behind the two men and sits next to Emilio on the bed.

Ay Dios, she says. Qué felicidad estar dentro de una casa ¡y con aire acondicionado!

John leaves and returns a few minutes later with two more sports drinks and clean towels. Drink these to replace lost salts while I make you up some food. Shower is through that door. I'll drive you to Tucson tomorrow morning and you can get a bus from there. If you want to make a phone call, there's a phone by the bed. He turns to leave and then turns back. What did you say her name was?

She's Matilde, Emilio says.

Mucho gusto, Matilde, John says.

Un placer, she says, and she finally smiles at him.

Do you have some water for your friend? I'm so thirsty.

He saw Pedro stumbling in the desert, desperate, his swollen purple tongue hanging from his mouth as he begged. His lips receding. His teeth protruding. He was in his final death throes.

I would do anything for a glass of cold water, friend, have you got one for me?

Here, he said, here, and he pulled the water directly from his own kidneys.

But Pedro had wandered off by then, the creosote plain spread out white and foreign before him, and Matilde was nowhere to be seen. Or was that her standing next to a bright blue barrel?

His kidneys pained him, his throat and mouth were filled with sand and stones. His arms and face pierced by the small thorns of the cacti.

You asked me why? Over the years I've seen hundreds of illegals running across the land and tearing it up and leaving piles of garbage and their feces and the drug runners and all the problems they are causing, driving across the desert at night without their lights on, abandoning cars all over this landscape, and the violence they bring, the destruction.

I used to think it was all their fault. Why do they bring their problems here? I'm a sixty-eight-year-old man who wishes it were different, wishes it were like it used to be when it was only the bighorn and owls and the coyotes and black hawks on my property. I have four grandchildren in Tucson: three, six, nine, and ten years old, and one of my boys married a Hispanic girl, so I have two half-Hispanic grandkids and I'm not a racist either. I only hate to see this place ruined.

My best answer is because none of us know what the future portends. One day it could be mine in a bad situation. And I'm an old man now who hopes that if that day should arrive and my son or grandson extends his arm for alms, his need apparent on him, the Samaritan will act foremost in accordance with his sacred duty.

The Record

August 2012

All literature consists of an effort to make life real.

Fernando Pessoa, *The Book of Disquiet*

Day 1. May 10.
Todos Santos. Huehuetenango. Xela. Tecún Umán. Tikal
Residence. 2,928 miles.

Days 2–3. May 11–12.
Tecún Umán. House of the Migrants. 2,928 miles.

Day 4. May 13.
Tapachula. Mexican hospitality. 2,905 miles.

Honduras is one of the poorest countries in Latin America
and holds the record for the highest homicide rate in
the world. Tegucigalpa has become the murder capital:
there are no areas of the city that are free of violent crime (17 bodies a day). Extortion by local trans-
national gangs (La Mara Salvatrucha and La Calle 18),
affect every level of society, estimates say upward of
90% of businesses must pay the "war tax," and most families pay it to live in their own homes. Since the military
coup in 2009 (tacitly supported by the U.S.), government
corruption has become even more pervasive. Government
agents, as well as the national police, are known collabo-
rators with international criminal organizations that now

run an approximate 90% of the world's cocaine production through Honduran territory on its way to U.S. markets. Impunity for crime hovers in the 95th percentile.

Throughout the Northern Triangle of Central America—Honduras, El Salvador, and Guatemala—high rates of violent crime, often instigated by gangs, corruption, abject poverty, weak states, weak judicial systems, impunity for crime, and climate change are causing people to flee. Often for their lives.

In the last five years, 55,000 migrants have died while attempting to cross Mexico. 20,000 Central Americans were kidnapped in Mexican territory in the last ten months alone.

Approximately 6,000 men, women, and children have died in the Sonoran Desert since the 1990s. Bodies are not easily found or counted, however, so this number is likely too low.

Dates and statistics don't affect people as much as a story, she says. You said you were going to tell what happened to us. You could begin it when you got on the bus in Todos Santos and end it in the desert. Try to remember all of it, I will help you with any details you forget.

A small history of migration to the North?

Yes, but so people will want to read it. Tell it as an adventure story and a romance and perhaps there is a tragedy at one moment.

I wanted to keep an accurate account, he says, not write a melodrama.

Stories tell the real history, they tell how it feels. The only question that remains is, how will it end?

Like this:

I take you to Muir Beach. We drive with my sister forty-five minutes to the coast from my house in Berkeley. We've been home over two months and we have mostly recovered. My mother likes you: you are kind and hardworking, you are staying in Susana's old room, and my mother knows you saved my life and so she also feels indebted to you. You have found work in a motel on University Avenue cleaning rooms and you are studying English at Berkeley Adult School at night. My mother and sisters respect your dedication to your children: you sent four hundred dollars home already and you have begun to pay my mother some of the money she sent us, which you insist on. And there is what we learned yesterday and await.

And then?

Antonia came to visit while you were at work. She was worried and I know she still loves me in her own way, but I am not that man any longer and you and I carried each other and we are bound. Antonia tried to understand, but I won't lie and say it was easy, I hurt her and this pain weighs on me, and I remain grateful for the way in which she also brought me home: her talisman did it. And although you won't like it as I say it here, I still care for her in my own manner, as I admire the person I was before I left and returned, but I am no longer him and she is not for me. And while I am not afraid all the time anymore, because I am home, I am still uncertain of our future. I am resuming my studies at UC Berkeley in two weeks. I've decided to declare a major in history instead of economics, and I've been considering a minor in film studies.

And then?

You are even more beautiful now. You have gained a little weight and you are not nervous all of the time and in your visage there is a brighter flush of life. The two brackets that hold your mouth do so with more ease, although you remain wary in a new country. And it still happens when you are near me: that electric pulse pushes out of you or from me toward you and back again. A closed circuit of love, desire, and fate. And you've called home and spoken with your mother and sister and you cried as you listened to your children's voices and they were saying Mami, when are you coming back? You told them in a little while, my love, and with this sadness on your chest you hung up the phone. You call two times a week, and each time it hurts you and you cry afterward and there is no easy balm for this pain. We do our best, as Pedro admonished us.

Because you also had to telephone Ana. You called her and you heard her wail across the distance. We all cried for Pedro in my living room in Berkeley in front of the bay window and the old oak tree outside it: my sisters, my mother, and me. My mother prays that his body will one day be recovered, and for Jonatan, for their souls, and you also called Jonatan's wife and asked if she had heard from him and she had not but she was hoping every day, she said, for a phone call letting her know he was okay. What will I do without him? she asked.

We arrived in downtown Oakland from Tucson on the Greyhound bus on the new moon, twenty-nine days after I left Todos Santos, the same amount of time it takes our satellite to complete its orbit around the earth. The stars shine less brightly here because of the light pollution than in the Mexican countryside: I could see the Big but not the Little Dipper in the sky.

There is good news: you called William's family in Tegucigalpa and learned that because William was only seventeen years old and an unaccompanied minor when he was apprehended, Border Patrol could not expedite his deportation. Immigration held him for a month and then he was released into the custody of his half-brother in New Jersey. He is safe and has begun attending high school and he has applied for political asylum with the help of an attorney.

We sit in the backseat and Brenda drives us over the cantilever bridge and you say again how lovely you find the San Francisco Bay. Mount Tam rises above everything in the distance, and the fog rests like a white canopy beyond the Golden Gate. You have one hand on my thigh and the other rests on your stomach.

You warned me this region was cold and cloud-covered in summer, but I don't mind it, you say. You pull your sweater closer into your body.

We drive along the eight-lane freeway in the low hills of Marin County. You are not used to the wide freeways and you still sharply notice the many large, shiny new cars on the road and the enormous homes and bright shopping centers and how clean and safe everything feels as long as you don't think about a policeman asking you for your identification papers. You twist your dark hair around your index finger and untwist and worry it when you see a patrol car on the highway.

Brenda maneuvers the car over the mountain pass and we can now see the ocean as we head down the narrow winding road toward the redwoods. When we reach the bottom of the hill near the small tavern called Pelican Inn, she turns left and drives to the parking lot and says she'll wait for us there.

You and I get out and we walk hand in hand toward the shore. This has been my favorite place since I was a boy, I tell you. The cliffs rise starkly above our heads and the gulls flying above us look as though they are resting on air, wings spread. A sliver of white moon leans against the light-blue sky and the fog encroaches and soon it will cover the scene. The beach is small and protected but even still it is cold here. There are dogs running up and down the sand at the water's edge. There are children screaming and dogs barking and running around.

I have it with me in my pocket. I have carried it in every pocket every day since I left Todos Santos, except for the time when we had no clothes and I held it in my hand and then beneath my tongue (so I could carry you). I have a superstition, although I am not a superstitious man: I must return it. I was able to come back, and so I must give it back to its place of origin. I take the white stone Antonia sent me five months ago when I was in jail and you watch me as I throw it into the sea.

I'd like to give you something, you say to me.

You have already given me everything, I say, and I look into your eyes and see again the light which continually draws me to you.

When the fog covers the sun, the beach becomes even colder and the wind stronger and we don't stay long after that. My sister turns the heat on high in the car as we drive back to the East Bay. Mom said she was making chicken and rice, Brenda says. My mother is still trying to fatten us up. She'd told us don't worry I'll hold dinner until you return and we can watch a movie together afterward if you'd like.

And when we both feel uncertain about what our future holds, then you tell me to have faith in God. Only He knows. And when we make love I see the world in you and although I am still not a believer, I believe in you and the stony dark earth, the dome of the sky, the silent gibbous moon, in human determination and even in some kind of hopefulness that we might carry. And in Las Patronas who give food to the unknown weary who pass by them each day on the cargo trains. In the fathers and volunteers at the Houses of the Migrants who provide the indigent travelers shelter, care, and nourishment on the road. In John Freedman of the Sonoran Desert who complied not with recent immigration statutes but with his own moral compass. In the old man with a bag of sweaters for strangers in Orizaba, the heavyset señora with the bean sandwiches at the depot, the boy with a bright orange in his hand held out to a poor and desperate traveler. The scared Mexican couple in Chiapas who gave five naked pilgrims their hospitality for the night. And the migrants on the trains who generously give what little they have, following the old ways in which food is always shared among the hungry, who cross the land tentative and hopeful that they might provide for and protect their families, save themselves, and via the good labor in a promised land, achieve something finer in their lifetimes.

And for my son.

For the child we learned of only yesterday at the doctor's office, a boy we did not plan for, conceived somewhere between the southern edge of the Sonoran Desert and the Bay Area of Northern California. We are scared, but we are in love, and we have to give it our best effort, for ourselves and for the boy who will be Mam and Chorotega, Spanish, and French. The mixing of the blood on this land continues. We are here, we remain, the new Americans.

Ay, Milo, this could be a great story!

But Mati, no one reads books anymore, so I've been thinking of making a movie instead.

THE END

Case ML 16-01403
Case Report ML 16-01403 Information

Identity: GARCIA, PEDRO GAITAN, male
Reporting Date: 2012-08-07
Corridor: Sasabe
Location: 3 miles southeast Arizona State Route 286/S. Sasabe Rd
Cause of Death: Exposure
OME Determined COD: PROBABLE HYPERTHERMIA
DUE TO EXPOSURE TO THE ELEMENTS
County: PIMA
State: Arizona

Case ML 16-01402
Case Report ML 16-01402 Information

Identity: Unidentified, male
Reporting Date: 2012-08-07
Corridor: Sasabe
Location: 3 miles southeast Arizona State Route 286/S. Sasabe Rd
Cause of Death: Exposure
OME Determined COD: PROBABLE HYPERTHERMIA
DUE TO EXPOSURE TO THE ELEMENTS
County: PIMA
State: Arizona

Case ML 16-01401
Case Report ML 16-01401 Information

Identity: Unidentified, female
Reporting Date: 2012-08-07
Corridor: Sasabe
Location: Arizona State Route 286 and Milepost 33
Cause of Death: Exposure
OME Determined COD: PROBABLE HYPERTHERMIA DUE TO EXPOSURE TO THE ELEMENTS
County: PIMA
State: Arizona

ACKNOWLEDGMENTS

Thank you to the Mills College Quigley Summer Grant for their support. To Carolina De Robertis and Cristina García, who each read an early draft. As always, to the band: Fowzia Karimi, Laleh Khadivi, Joel Tomfohr, Ed Ntiri, Keenan Norris, and Muthoni Kiarie. Karen Bouris and Rob Hilbun for their early enthusiasm. Paula Merwin, stalwart lover of books, who during the many years it took this novel to find final form passed on, rest in peace, friend. Mil gracias Victoria Sanford for a journey she undertook with a stranger in Guatemala over a decade ago and whose friendship has been its ongoing gift. Susan Schulman for believing in this book from its earliest draft and standing by it until it saw publication. To Emily Graff, for your support and enthusiasm from our very first phone conversation, and Lashanda Anakwah: thank you. Guilio Celotto for a last minute translation of Dante. Always to SJ.

ABOUT THE AUTHOR

Micheline Aharonian Marcom was born in Saudi Arabia and raised in Los Angeles. She has published seven novels, including a trilogy about the Armenian genocide and its aftermath in the twentieth century. Marcom splits her time between California and Virginia, where she teaches creative writing at the University of Virginia. She is the founder and creative director of the New American Story Project (NASP), a living archive of voices exploring the forces of migration and the lives of new Americans. Visit NASP at newamericanstoryproject.org.